George and the Stolen Sunny Spot

Kristin Bauer Ganoung

Text Copyright © 2017 Kristin Bauer Ganoung
Illustration and Cover Design © 2017 Lisa Bohart
Interior Design © 2017 by Polaris Studio

Published by Prairieland Press
PO Box 2404
Fremont, NE 68026-2404
Printed in the U.S.A.

Publisher's Cataloging-in-Publication data

Names: Ganoung, Kristin Bauer.
Title: George and the stolen sunny spot / Kristin Bauer Ganoung.
Description: Fremont, NE: Prairieland Press, 2017.
Identifiers: ISBN 978-1-944132-04-0 (pbk.) | 978-1-944132-05-7 (ebook) |
LCCN 2016952322
Summary: George, the feline chief of farm security, tries to prevent a younger cat
and a pair of dogs from stealing his favorite napping spot.
Subjects: LCSH Cats—Juvenile fiction. | Dogs—Juvenile fiction. | Friendship—
Fiction. | Farm life—Fiction. | BISAC JUVENILE FICTION / Animals / General
| JUVENILE FICTION / Animals / Farm Animals | JUVENILE FICTION /
Social Themes / Friendship
Classification: LCC PZ7 .G151 Ge 2016 | [Fic]—dc23.

Prairieland Press™

To Dad and Mom,
who always thought I could
and kept prodding until I did.

Contents

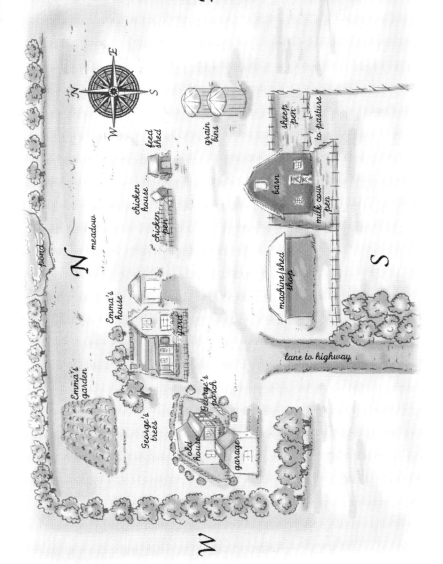

Chapter One
Garden Patrol

Nobody told me that my favorite napping spot was in danger of a hostile takeover until it was too late. I suppose I shouldn't be surprised—about not being told, that is. For some reason, humans feel no need to share valuable information with a cat, even if the cat is in charge of farm security like I am.

By the way, my name's George—a.k.a. "that troublemaker, George" to the humans involved. 'Course the only reason there was trouble was because the porch was mine in the first place, but somehow that fact was overlooked in all of the ruckus, rumpus, and general uproar.

The funny thing was that the brouhaha began quietly enough. After all, it was just an ordinary summer morning, and I was doing an ordinary garden patrol with Emma.

"George."

What? I shoved even closer to Emma's legs with ears pricked and whiskers twitching. Had she spotted a grasshopper on one of the green bean plants she was picking? I still couldn't see the varmint, so I wedged my head under her fingers to give the leaves a more careful examination.

"*George.*"

Emma's hand tried to brush me back onto the path between the plants, and I dutifully looked in that direction, but there were obviously no grasshoppers there. Grasshoppers like hiding in the leaves, not out in the open. But being only a human, maybe Emma didn't realize that. I squeezed between her knees and searched underneath the plant where she was working. I wasn't seeing anything here, either, but Emma kept saying my name.

"George, you fur ball."

A fur ball? I quickly glanced down at my side. No, my orange, tiger-striped fur was behaving itself. No tangles or poof in evidence. Maybe Emma's eyesight was going bad.

"George!"

I laid back my ears. Hey, lady, you don't need to

shout. I'm not deaf, you know, and I'm being as thorough as I can.

Emma stood, leaving the area in front of me wide open. There! That was more like it. Now I'd see the critter for sure, and…

Whoa!

Suddenly I was lifted off the ground. The tops of the bean bushes went rushing by under my nose. Then the lettuce row, and finally the fence. Emma dropped me over the side and I landed, on all four feet of course, with tail flicking.

This was the third time I'd found myself on this side of the fence today. I looked back for Emma, but she'd already returned to the green beans and was crouched beside them again. Still flicking my tail, I sat and thought. She'd called my name, but she didn't want my help with grasshoppers. What then?

Gophers maybe? I glanced around the outside of the fence. No, I'd looked for them yesterday. No trace of an invasion. Hmmm.

Coon tracks? No, too early in the season for coons.

I scratched at an ear with my back paw. There was no getting around it. I'd have to go back into the garden one more time. Emma wasn't a very good communicator.

With her for a boss, being chief in charge of farm security required a lot of patience. But duty was duty.

I stood and had gathered myself for a leap to the top of the fence when the rumble and rattle of a vehicle coming up our lane reached my ears. I paused and looked in the direction of the houses. Sure enough, a dusty, faded blue pickup was crunching through the gravel into the farm yard.

As the pickup came to a stop, Emma stood and waved at the people in the cab with so much enthusiasm that if she'd been a dog, I'm sure her tail would've whapped those green bean plants to shreds. Good thing Emma didn't have a tail.

The two people in the pickup, a man and a woman, waved back at her, then got out and started walking in our direction. Hmm. I'd never seen these particular humans before, so why was Emma being so friendly?

Then the new lady spotted me. "Here kitty, kitty," she cooed, bending down as if to touch me.

I poofed my orange fur and showed her my fangs. Kitty indeed. I was a seasoned professional. Couldn't she see the notch out of one of my ears? That was from a brawl with a rat, thank you very much. I was definitely *not* kitty material.

The lady pulled back her hand.

Emma had come out of the garden by now, and she frowned at me. "George, behave yourself," she said. Then she gave each of those strangers a big hug, as if they were long-lost pals or something.

Humph. Humans. You try to protect them and all they have to say is 'behave yourself.' I stalked off in the direction of the houses. My services were obviously no longer needed here.

"That's an awful big cat," the new lady said as I left.

"Yeah, that's George," said Emma. I didn't even need to look back at her to know she was probably standing with her hands on her hips watching me. "He's tough as old leather with an attitude a mile long. It may take him awhile to get used to you."

Used to them? I looked over my shoulder. That didn't bode well. Were they sticking around for the day, or two or three?

I shuddered as visions of the farm's last visitor played through my head. Emma's niece had come for her entire week of spring vacation. If she'd actually hung around the house and minded her own business, it would've been no problem. But for some reason, she watched me going on patrol around the barn and got this crazy idea that I would look cute dressed up like a princess.

A princess!!

That evening she caught me right outside of the sheep pen, and the entire flock of sheep with Pauline, their llama guard, had watched as she popped me into a pink frilly dress with a tiara dangling over an eyebrow. I'd had to unsheathe my claws and do some serious damage to the dress before the little whippersnapper would take it off of me.

The sheep, of course, had then gossiped about the incident with every pigeon and sparrow who happened to fly by, and those bird brains had spread it to the neighboring farms. It'd taken *months* to live that one down.

Not only that, but Emma had given me a good "talking to" after the blow-up and made me spend the night in the garage without supper, even though I'd been very careful not to damage the kid along with the dress. That's the kind of thanks I get.

In any case, I was wary of humans who called me "kitty" and acted as if they might stay for a prolonged visit. Right then and there, I decided that my house was needing an emergency inspection. So I picked up my pace and high-tailed it out of there. Not that I was scared or anything, but duty was definitely calling.

I passed by Emma and Ted's house first. Big, brick affair with tidy flower beds tucked here and there under the trees and by the white fence. Nice enough house, I guess, but nothing to compare to *my* house.

I crossed the gravel driveway, slinking by those strangers' blue pickup, and arrived at the other abode on the farm. My house. Two stories tall, paint chipping off the white siding, grass a little tall and unkempt, the gate sagging on its hinges. Just perfect. Especially with the huge porch that stretched completely across the front of the house.

I bounded up the porch steps and peered through the gaps in the floorboards. Nope. No sign of rodent intruders down there. I walked over to the old screen door and sniffed around the edges. No spiders or mice taking up residence today.

Perfect. That meant more time for napping, and after a garden patrol like today, I was in serious need of a nap.

On the far side of the porch, a beam of sunlight was shining down through a hole in the roof and splashing onto the floorboards below. I settled into the perfectly warmed puddle on the worn wood and half-closed my eyes, enjoying the feeling of almost-sleep before it settled into full slumber.

Ah. This was the life. My porch. Cat heaven.

My thoughts drifted back to that grand moment when the porch had truly become all mine—when Emma had passed by on her way to the garden and noticed me rodent-hunting under the weathered floorboards. "George, you're an extermination machine," she said. "Your place has fewer rodents than anywhere else in the neighborhood."

My whiskers twitched at the memory. She'd said "*Your* place." That meant my house, my yard, my porch.

It was only fair, of course, because I'd been doing all the work. The house'd been sitting vacant since Ted's mom had decided the stairs were getting too much for her old legs to climb and that she needed to move into town. And anyone knows that an empty house is an open invitation for pesty freeloaders. I'd figured that if a family of rodents moved in, they'd be on the lookout for other locations to colonize, too, which was a security issue for the entire farm.

It was obviously a job for chief in charge of farm

security. *Me.* So I'd single-handedly stopped a gopher invasion of the lawn, rid the porch of a community of crickets, and put a halt to the migration of mice under the porch. Yep, it was only fair that Emma had given the old place to me.

I slid my eyes fully closed and commenced to dreaming. It was a beautiful dream. Emma was opening cans and cans of expensive cat food and serving it to me on fancy platters.

Suddenly the can opener from my dreams developed a peculiar squeak that shivered my fur and made my claws twitch. I turned over, snapped open my eyes, and realized that it was the gate to my yard that was squeaking. It took my dream-numbed brain a few seconds to process the mob of people trooping up the sidewalk in my direction. Emma, Ted—and those two strangers.

Emma was the first up the steps. She nudged me with her boot. "Out of the way, George," she said, leading the passel of people through the front door— *my* front door.

I sneezed into the dust on the porch and scowled. Trespassers.

Padding over to the screen door, I swiveled my ears

to monitor what was happening inside.

"…dusty…cobwebs." I heard the new lady's voice trailing from somewhere within.

"But it's solid as ever…sturdy construction." That had to be Ted talking.

"And it can easily be cleaned," Emma said, as she appeared around a corner. "The place has been neglected for much too long."

Neglected! I laid down my ears. Speak for yourself, lady. I'd worked hard to keep the local rodents from setting up camp.

I narrowed my eyes at the intruders as they came out of the screen door and filed past me. The new lady paused and looked down at me again, wiggling her fingers a bit as though she just couldn't wait to stick a bow on my head. I poofed my tail and hissed. Loudly.

Emma turned and glared at me, but I didn't back down. No way was I going to be a pink princess again. I had a reputation to maintain if I wanted the rodents to do more than fall over laughing when they saw me.

"Sorry about that, Lil," said Emma. "Just stay out of his way for now. He'll eventually calm down."

"He's a *lot* bigger than Felix," the 'Lil' lady said, still staring at me. She drew her eyebrows down exactly the way Emma does when she's not happy.

"Yes, he certainly is a large cat," Emma agreed.

"Too many kibbles," Ted said, and the entire group of humans laughed.

I laid back my ears and stalked off the porch. There was not an ounce of fat on this sleek body—it was all muscle and claws. See if I'd stick around and be the brunt of any more bad jokes.

I'd squeezed through the lilac bushes in the back yard and was nearly into the row of trees behind them when I caught a scrap of Lil's voice. "... Felix ... get along together." I stopped to listen but couldn't hear any more human conversation.

Later that evening I wandered back to my house and found the strange vehicle gone. Good riddance. Surely that was the end of that nonsense.

If only I'd known.

Chapter Two
Intruder Alert

When I woke up the next morning, the angle of the sun shining through the dusty window in Emma's garage told me that I'd probably missed the morning milking and Pauline's departure with the sheep for their day in the pasture *and* some of garden patrol, too. Emma was likely fit to be tied, wondering where I was.

I wasn't in any hurry, though. I *stretched* from the tops of my ears to the tips of my toes, and then lay back in my nest of old bath towels, reliving last night's patrol.

Ted had been complaining about mice droppings on his work bench in the machine shed, and I'd taken that to be extermination orders. I'd set up camp behind Ted's baler last night, and stayed there motionless until it felt like my muscles were permanently frozen in position. But it was all worth it when I'd seen little whiskers peeking from a crack in the wall behind the work bench.

When all was said and done, I'd strolled back to the garage with a plump, corn-fed mouse in my belly. By that time, the moon had already floated its way across the entire sky and was hiding behind the rows of trees to the west of the farm yard. It was late, late, late. But duty was duty, no matter what the hour. And my mission had been a success.

Which was why I didn't feel guilty at all about sleeping late.

After I'd given myself a thorough whisker-washing, I checked out my food bowl, but there was nothing but the economy-style kibbles that Emma leaves for me. I wrinkled my nose and twitched my whiskers downward. In the garden right now, Emma was probably scaring up crickets and grasshoppers while she weeded. They'd make a much more interesting breakfast.

As I ambled across the driveway though, I could feel my sunny spot calling to me. Change of plans. I'd start my morning patrol there.

I was just coiling my muscles to spring over the fence when a sudden movement on the old porch caught my eye. I froze. There in *my* spot on *my* porch was another cat. A youngish, smallish, gray-striped cat sleeping in *my* spot!

My fur poofed, and the muscles in my back contracted into an arch. While I'd been sleeping, Emma had snuck another cat onto the farm! But then my super-tuned powers of observation fixed itself on one of the details: gray. This new cat was gray. Emma would never replace me with a gray cat.

I sat and licked the disturbed fur on my own orange tail to calm myself. This must be some kind of emergency, I finally decided. The kid must be lost and figured this looked like a good place to take shelter. No problem. I would be glad to help.

I sleeked my ears with a paw and did a graceful leap to the top of the fence. The top board of the fence creaked under me, and the new cat's eyes snapped open. He didn't move.

"Hello, kid," I called, as I jumped from the fence and strolled to the porch. "My name's George. I'm chief of security for this place, and it appears to me—"

"Go away," the new cat interrupted. He flopped

over, turning his back toward me.

I halted with one paw on the bottom step, my mouth hanging open. This boy was in desperate need of some manners. Quickly, I brought myself back to attention. "No can do. Like I said, I'm chief of security here. Gotta investigate any and all strangers. So what's your name, Son?"

There was another moment of silence.

My whiskers twitched downward. It appeared I'd need to get close enough to look the youngster in the eye. If he needed a lesson in respect, I was highly qualified to teach it. I jumped up the first couple of steps.

The kid must've heard me coming closer. He didn't turn around, but he finally spoke. "My name's Felix. Just leave off with the speeches and get out of here, okay? You're interrupting my nap."

Well. I hadn't had to deal with such out-and-out rudeness since the pink princess incident.

I laid back my ears. "Perhaps I'm not making myself clear. As the chief in charge of this location, I have the authority to dispose of all intruders. And right now, pip-squeak, you are in *my* spot on *my* porch. If you won't cooperate, I'm prepared to give you your marching orders the hard way."

I waited for that Felix cat to snap to attention, but all he gave was a shoulder twitch.

"You've been given bad information," he said, still directing his words to the wall. "This is now *my* spot. So get lost."

OOOOOH. The time for talking politely was obviously over. I *would* have to pound a lesson into him, and I was confident of the outcome. After all, I was at least ten pounds heavier and had several cat/bat/rat fights under my belt. (Also one skunk battle, but I don't need to explain what happened with that one.)

"OK, have it your way," I hissed, preparing to spring.

Then I heard a sound that made all my orange hairs stand up on end. I froze except for my finely tuned ears, which were swiveling quickly to pinpoint the source of the noise. Ever so carefully I turned my head and caught sight of two slavering, growling dogs standing beside the porch, their glinting eyes pointed right at me.

Instantly, I turned tail and bolted back to the fence. As soon as I moved, the dogs rushed after me, baying and snapping as if cat-on-the-lam was their favorite breakfast dish.

I leapt up and over the fence, sped to the corner of the brick house and clawed my way to the top of the nearest tree. Only then did I look back. My pursuers were still in the yard where I'd left them, howling and raising a terrible ruckus.

What was going on around here? All I did was sleep late, and now the entire farmyard was invaded! Thank goodness the gate was shut, although it did occur to me to wonder why. Strangers don't usually wander into a farmyard and lock themselves in.

Hmm. Unless the dogs were working together to trap that cheeky Felix cat. I almost felt sorry for him then. The dogs would be sure to go after him next, and the kid obviously had no fighting experience.

"Run, stupid!" I shouted at him. "Get outta there! You're next!!"

As I figured, the canines sniffed around and then loped over to the porch. By now, the little guy was sitting up. But instead of hissing and spitting at the approaching danger, he stretched and began to lick his paws.

"Idiot!" I hollered. "Aren't you smart enough to

know certain death when it breathes on you?!"

But instead of attacking the little upstart, the dogs moseyed up the steps, tongues lolling, and snuffled at him. Then they dropped down, one on either side of him, resting their heads on their paws in perfect synchrony.

Felix tilted his nose and looked straight into the tree where I was sitting with my fur sticking out at all angles. His ears were twitching. He was laughing at me!

"Good job, Brutus," he said in an unnecessarily loud voice to the sleek brown Boxer lying next to him.

"Thanks, Boss," said the Boxer.

Then he turned to the long-eared Basset hound whose tongue was dribbling puddles on the wood. "Excellent show, Festus."

"Thanks, Boss," said the Basset.

The kid cozied up between the two of them and closed his eyes.

I slunk under a screening of leaves and began shredding the bark of the nearest limb with my claws. That puny pipsqueak wasn't going to get the better of *me*. This was *my* farm, and that was *my* spot, and when Emma heard those barking dogs, she'd be out of the garden in a split second to chase off the unwanted strays.

I waited.

And waited.

But Emma didn't appear.

I finally hooked my claws into the tattered bark and licked the fur on my shoulders until it was flat. Good. Now I could think calmly again.

I turned my attention back to the old house and yard and studied the layout. Soon my eagle-sharp eyes began to notice some other oddities. Not only was the gate shut, it had been straightened and rehung. The sidewalk was swept. The screen door to the house was propped open. There was a strange pickup in the driveway…

No, wait. It wasn't a strange pickup—it was that old, smelly pickup I'd seen yesterday! That could only mean…

Those humans were back. They were working on the old house. They must be moving in!

No wonder Emma wasn't running from the garden to find out what the ruckus meant. No wonder that Felix cat had the idea he belonged here.

I narrowed my eyes and stared down at him with a look so cold that he should've turned into a kitty icicle right then and there. Felix, my boy, you are so wrong,

I growled to myself. I can't do much about the humans inside of the house, but that porch is mine. I'm the senior officer around here, and I'm in charge. Dogs or no dogs, it's my duty to help you figure that out.

Chapter Three
Battle Lost, Porch Regained— for the Moment

I sat in that tree for a couple of hours, flicking my tail and watching the porch through narrowed eyes. My tail-swishing eventually caught the attention of a resident squirrel who started chittering insults. "You call *that* skinny little thing a tail?" and "Better find a lower branch if you want it to hold someone *your* size," and "I'll bet you're slower than my baby sister blindfolded and going backwards!"

I tried to ignore him, but pretty soon those canines got up and wandered over to the fence. They put their front paws on the links and added to the racket with some yappity-yap of their own.

"Hey, orange cat, that squirrel *does* have a better looking tail. Come on over and we'll fluff it for you a little more."

And then that little Felix cat—from *my* spot on *my* porch—opened his eyes, looked straight up into the tree at me, and wrinkled his nose in what looked to be a huge grin.

Okay, okay, I know that losing your temper is a very unprofessional thing to do, but at that point, I'd had it with being Mr. Nice Guy. My fur was definitely ruffled. I charged after the closest source of annoyance, which happened to be the squirrel. He was sitting three or four branches down from me, and by the time I'd clawed my way there, he'd scampered to a lower limb and was chattering his rude remarks even more loudly.

The dogs were still yapping and yukking it up, and I thought I'd surely go deaf. But I couldn't back down at this point because that little feline thief on the porch was still watching me. OOOH, I wished I could wipe that smug look off his face.

I lit after the squirrel again instead. He scampered down to the base of the tree and took off across the lawn, heading to the nearest power pole with me in hot pursuit.

Suddenly a blast of cold water hit me in the face.

Yow! Half blinded, I screeched to a halt on the slippery grass, did an about face, and scrambled back to the tree. I clawed my way to one of the top limbs and flattened myself behind a cover of leaves before brushing the water out of my eyes. The first thing I saw was Lil standing by the front gate, one hand on Brutus's head and the other holding a garden hose. She was staring up at me through the greenery.

"Bad kitty," she hollered. "You leave that poor little squirrel alone."

From his perch on the power pole, the squirrel was staring at me, too. He chittered, "Yeah, you bad kitty. Leave the poor little squirrel alone!" Then he turned and flicked his tail at me before racing across the power line to the roof of the house and out of sight.

I flattened my ears and glared at the Lil lady. Poor squirrel? The woman was obviously delusional, not to mention downright rude. It must be a family trait, passed from animal to human, or maybe the other way around.

"Here, Brutus. Here, Festus," Lil called over her shoulder as she walked to the porch. She rubbed their ears and laughed when they tried to jump up and lick her face. Then she pushed the dogs down and climbed up the steps to my spot. She scooped Felix into her arms and sat down with him, petting and rubbing and pushing the dogs away when their noses got too close.

I couldn't believe it. She was taking the word of a conniving squirrel, two slobbery, dim-witted canines, and a feline con artist over *me,* a hired security professional. From my perch on the branch, I scowled at all the drooly devotion going on below me. But I'd just been given a vital piece of information. That pipsqueak, Felix, had the dogs *and* this human wrapped around his tiny toes. Whatever I did, it would have to be an undercover operation.

I glanced around the area. No one was watching me since every animal in the vicinity was slobbering over Lil. Now was the time for retreat. I slipped out of the tree and stealthily made my way to home base, Emma's garage. I had some serious planning to do.

It didn't take me long to decide that I needed more information. I'd been caught off guard, and the situation had gotten completely out of control. I needed to do a little spying to make sure no other surprises were in store.

So I spent the afternoon skulking around the old house, which was an easy enough assignment. There are plenty of overgrown bushes and trees along the perimeter for cover, and my expertise at stalking and spying is widely known. Just ask any rodent who is unfortunate enough to find himself in my territory.

There wasn't much to see though. Felix and his canine muscle men stayed on the porch, while Lil and Jason, and occasionally Emma, went in and out of the house with buckets, ladders, and rags. It was starting to get dark when the two new humans loaded up the animals in their smelly pickup and left in a cloud of dust.

Good riddance. I hoped they'd never come back. But I knew that was just wishful thinking.

I climbed up onto my precious porch and looked around. Felix's food and water bowls were still there, and I stuck my nose inside—just to look for clues, of course—but they were empty. I curled up in my sunny spot—no sun left at the moment, unfortunately—and got ready to take a much-deserved snooze.

Then I remembered I still had to do an evening report with Pauline. Being a llama, Pauline is extra sensitive to the presence of intruders, which is why she does such an excellent job of guarding the sheep out in the pasture during the day. And in the evening, after she's got them safely back into the corral by the barn, she gives me a perimeter report, letting me know of any security alerts she may have detected while on duty.

Tonight, of course, I was thinking more about my favorite napping spot than unwanted critters in the pasture. But being a good security chief, I couldn't skip her report. I twitched my whiskers downward, heaved myself from my comfortable position, and stalked across the porch, heading for the corrals next to the barn.

Punctual as always, Pauline was standing by the gate waiting for me.

I got right to the point. "Any intruders spotted on patrol?"

She looked down her nose at me, but I wasn't offended. She looks down her nose at everyone. "No, but you need to take a look at the gopher population. It's getting out of control."

Great. A lot of things were suddenly getting out of control. I sat on the stubbly grass and huffed into my whiskers. Duty was duty, after all.

"I'll go out early tomorrow morning and take a look down a few holes," I said, getting to my feet. My spot on the porch was calling me.

She nodded. "Wait for me before you head out."

I halted in mid step. "Trouble?"

"Nothing I've actually seen, but…" She looked over her shoulder toward the pasture.

"You think Old Mangy might be back."

Her nostrils twitched, and she looked down her nose at me again. "Things have been a little too quiet. Something is keeping the local wild turkey population from wandering through."

I narrowed my eyes. Old Mangy was a coyote with a bad reputation in these parts. He was cagey enough to make off with a lamb while your back was turned. Not that Pauline's back was ever turned, but I was still nervous. No small animal was safe while he was around—including me.

I gave myself a shake. Being chief of security was a dangerous job. I'd known that when I'd been hired, and the risks hadn't changed. "I'll see you bright and early then."

Pauline nodded once and turned back to the sheep without any further chitchat, which was fine by me. I had some serious napping to do before the invaders returned.

Chapter Four
Aunt Eloise

I started back to my spot on the porch, but suddenly realized that I wasn't the least bit sleepy. My mind was too busy working overtime on what to do about Felix, his bevy of bodyguards, *and* Old Mangy. Maybe some serious rodent chasing would calm me down. And lucky for me, at just that moment I was stalking right past the barn. Perfect rodent territory.

Now the barn isn't really mine to patrol. It belongs to the barn cat, my Aunt Eloise, who retired there after many long years of being chief of security. I generally stay out of her way, being that she and I have very different ideas about how a farm should be run.

Since it was evening, however, I'd be perfectly safe. Aunt Eloise no longer did night patrols. She'd informed me of that herself when I'd asked for a little help with some wayward 'possums who'd snuck into the feed shed last spring.

"No more sitting in dark corners going cross-eyed for me," she'd said.

Yeah, right, I thought. What she meant was no more cat-nap interruptions in the middle of the night. And she was always complaining about *me* being lazy. Still, I wouldn't have to worry about her ruining a good prowl.

I squeezed through a narrow gap under the barn's closed door into the dark, cool interior. Swiveling my ears, I made a careful sweep of the closest set of stalls. Silence. I padded soundlessly over the hard packed dirt floor to the feed room, figuring that's where the mice would be hiding out.

I crept onto the wood floor of the feed room and paused, surveying the room with my ultra-sharp night vision. My eyes fastened onto a black shape crouched in the corner. No, not black. The hair coat was dusty gray and patchy. Too big for a mouse…

Oh, no—it couldn't be! Turning, I tried to beat a hasty (and silent) retreat.

"Georgie!" a shrill voice called from behind me. My whiskers went rigid.

I forced my fur back under control then slowly turned. "Yes, Aunt Eloise?"

"Georgie, come on over here and sit a spell. Haven't seen you around for a while."

I shut my eyes and concentrated on keeping my ears from flattening before I dutifully padded over to sit next to her.

She squinted her cloudy eyes at me. "You need to come around more often, Georgie. The mice in this barn are getting cheeky, and I can't seem to keep up on my own like I used to."

"Yes, Aunt Eloise."

She wobbled to her feet and almost toppled over into a pile of feed sacks sitting nearby. I quickly wedged my shoulder against her sharp rib bones to keep her upright. She swished her nearly hairless tail into my face, seemingly unaware of my help. "Now, if *my* George were still here, he'd have the place in proper order. Yes, he would. No slacker was he. Why, did I ever tell you about the time he caught—"

"Three gophers in one hour." I said the words around her tail. "One right after the other."

"Like clockwork, he was," Aunt Eloise finished. "Old fashioned sense of duty. Not like these young cats nowadays." She turned to nip at a mosquito that'd homed in on her ear.

My whiskers twitched downward and I muttered, "Yeah, and it was that overdone sense of duty that got Uncle George killed." After all, no cat in his right mind would patrol the pasture alone after dark, which means Uncle George must've been at least half crazy when he gave it a try.

"What?" My aunt leaned into me until her whiskers brushed across my nose. I sneezed. Dust went flying everywhere.

Aunt Eloise rolled her eyes. "Now every mouse in the barn will know we're here. How many years will it take you to master silent stalking, my dear boy?"

I bit my tongue and squashed a half dozen less-than-polite words. "Right, Aunt Eloise. I'll keep practicing. Now I need to finish the evening patrol. See you later!"

Much later.

I squeezed out from underneath her, and she settled with a plop of dust onto the floor.

"Georgie, you be back here tomorrow morning, you hear? I need your help cornering some of these rodents!"

"Yeah, sure. No problem." I trotted out of the room

and made a beeline for the crack under the barn door.

"I'll be expecting you!" she hollered after me, her voice piercing through the gloom.

I slid out into the open air and took a deep breath. Wonderful. How was I going to get rid of that Felix cat if I had to go chase gophers and *then* be trapped in the barn with Aunt Eloise? I squeezed my eyes shut and shook my head. Aunt Eloise and the barn mice would have to wait. My most important assignment was to get rid of Felix and his guards—permanently.

Chapter Five
Running for Cover

I tossed and turned in my nest of old towels all night long, and when the sun finally came up, I still didn't have a clue about how to get that Felix cat alone. Even worse, the smelly pickup came growling up the driveway, this time pulling a trailer, just as I was doing my morning stretches in preparation for bathing and then breakfast.

I unsheathed my claws and shredded a corner of my bedding. I hadn't even been able to have a proper nap in my sunny spot last night because, of course, being night there'd been no sun. And now that there was finally some sun…

I peeked out from under the garage door, which Emma leaves cracked open for me, then flattened my ears as I watched the two hounds jump out of the pickup cab and nip and growl and chase each other up the porch steps. Felix didn't bother to jump out with them. He had a nice ride to the porch, all snuggled up in Lil's arms.

Softie. If it weren't for those canines, I'd have no problem sending him packing.

Suddenly I was no longer hungry for dry kibble. I really wanted to *chase* something. Skipping my bath, I headed over to the corrals. I'd accompany Pauline to the pasture and give those gophers a run for their money.

But when I got there, the sheep were milling around inside the fence with the gate closed. It was still early enough that Emma hadn't let them out yet. And after Pauline's warning last night, I wasn't wanting to go out to the pasture by myself. Now don't get me wrong—I wasn't scared. I just wasn't stupid, either.

I pulled my whiskers down and stalked over to the grain bins to patrol there instead. Usually there were lots of catchable mice in that area. Good, fat ones.

Evidently I wasn't the only one in the mood for a good chase, however. As I was slipping through the bushy weeds that grew around the tall, round metal bins, I heard grass swishing violently behind me. I spun around. Two huge shadows were lunging after me.

The dogs! Some idiot had let them out of the yard.

I knew I was in trouble. There wasn't a tree within dashing distance, and I couldn't climb the slick sides of the bin. I was forced into Plan B. I arched my back and puffed my fur, trying to look as big as possible while hissing and showing my fangs. Maybe those big bruisers would believe I was too dangerous to take on in a fight.

The dogs stopped when they saw me all puffed up like that. They crossed around in front of me, sniffing the ground and acting like they'd just come over for polite conversation. They stayed out of range of my claws, though.

I kept my back to the grain bins and flattened my ears, doing my best to look like a ball of deadly fangs and claws. Unfortunately, the brutes weren't taking the warning. Instead, they halted and curled their lips, exposing their own fangs. Brutus began to growl low in his throat, and Festus joined in with some yapping.

"Attack!" Brutus suddenly howled.

I thought I was a goner for sure and had just unsheathed my claws for the final battle, when I heard Lil call, "Brutus, Festus, breakfast time!"

She must've been serving something better than cat meat. The dogs immediately went silent, looked at each other, and took off toward the house. I stayed puffed up and dangerous-looking for a few seconds longer, then bounded off to the garage as fast as I could go just in case those dogs changed their minds about what they wanted for breakfast.

I almost ran smack into Emma as she came out of the brick house, carrying her metal milking pail.

Emma!

She would have the authority (in other words, the size) to get those intruders out of my territory. After all, she was the one who'd given the porch and yard to me. All I had to do was get her over to the yard. She would see the trespassers immediately and restore me to full command.

I popped my tail straight into the air and rubbed against her jeans. She obviously figured that was my way of asking for a back scratch because she bent down and gave me one. I rubbed a little harder, trying to communicate that I had something important on my mind. However, she just nudged me out of the way with her foot and made a beeline to the barn.

I tried to point her in the direction of the old house

by twining around her legs, but instead of taking the hint and turning in the other direction, she almost tripped. One of her feet planted itself on my tail. I yowled and scrabbled out of the way.

"George," she said without the least trace of sympathy, "get your hairy self out from underfoot."

She started toward the barn again. This time I galloped in front of her, trying to block her path. I purred and rubbed her shins and did my best to guide her back toward the old place.

"George," she said, using the same warning tone that she uses when I'm on her lap during garden patrol.

Knowing what usually happens when she says my name in that way, I should have given it up and moved out of range of her foot. But I was feeling a little desperate. I was hoping for a snooze on the porch before garden patrol. I stood on my hind legs and leaned against her, giving her my best 'I need some help' stare and batting at her arm with my paw.

She wasn't having any of it. She pushed me down and gave me a good solid jab with her foot. "Out of the way, George. At this rate I won't get the milking done until lunch time."

I stared after her, feeling my tail and whiskers

droop. This was unbelievable. Here she'd hired me to protect the place, and now she was callously ignoring me. I followed her into the barn at a distance. Maybe when she walked back to the house, she would look across the driveway and detect the problem.

While waiting for her to finish milking, I hunkered down and peered through the crack under the barn door, keeping an eye on the canine situation. The dogs were nowhere in sight, but the gate was still open. The fur on my tail poofed and I cocked my ears forward, straining for any clue of their whereabouts.

"Out of the way, George."

I jumped as Emma strode up behind me. She nudged me with her boot, slid open the door and stepped through. Before I could gather my thoughts, she'd pulled the door shut again and was gone.

Wait! I bunched my muscles to squeeze under the door and bound after her. I had to get her to notice the invasion of my property! But suddenly I was distracted by a scent wafting through the air, curling around me in Emma's wake.

Fresh milk.

The rich, warm smell of it put every other thought from my mind. I looked over my shoulder toward the feed room, but there was no sign of Aunt Eloise. Silently, I padded to the stall at the opposite end of the barn where Emma did the milking.

Just as I suspected. Emma had left some milk in a dish for Aunt Eloise.

I hesitated. Emma doesn't bring any milk out to the garage. She says Eloise needs the milk to fatten her up a bit, but that I'm plenty fat already. That's total nonsense, of course. There's not an ounce of fat on this body—it's sheer muscle.

No. I shook my head. It's Aunt Eloise's breakfast. Besides, I knew how tired I get when my stomach's full. I didn't have time for a nap right now.

Still I hesitated, one paw hovering in the air. Both my evening and morning hunts had been interrupted, and I was on the verge of starving to death! Surely it wouldn't hurt to take just a couple of sips. I'd leave enough for Aunt Eloise. I wouldn't fill myself up…. But before I knew it, there was only a dribble of milk left.

Huh. I stared at the almost empty dish. Emma must have been stingy with the milk this morning. I glanced behind my shoulder, on alert for Aunt Eloise's wobbly footsteps. What was I going to do? I'd eaten all of her breakfast.

I'd better catch a mouse for her as a peace offering.

I prowled the perimeter, avoiding the feed room, then skulked over to the ladder leading to the loft. My eyelids began to feel a little heavy. I shook the cobwebs out of my head. No time for a nap now.

The ladder, however, seemed unusually tall today. By the time I reached the top, my feet felt as heavy as if they'd each picked up a few inches of sticky mud. I could hardly pull myself over to the nearest heap of hay.

A little snooze couldn't hurt, I reasoned. It's still early in the day. Pauline and the sheep haven't left for the pasture yet. I have plenty of time to find a mouse and then get Emma over to the old yard to take care of the intruders before I'm needed for backup in Pauline's territory.

I carefully washed the milk off my whiskers and lay down for a short cat nap. Well, I'd planned on it being short. But when I woke up, I could tell by the angle of the sun peering in through the grimy panes of the loft window that I'd slept much longer than intended. The morning was slipping away, and so was my chance to get Felix rooted out of my spot in time for my afternoon snooze!

Chapter Six
Out of the Frying Pan
and into the Fire

Good grief! I'd have to wait till later to catch a mouse for Aunt Eloise. I needed to waylay Emma before she headed back from the garden for lunch, and then there was the gopher problem to take care of for Pauline. I was definitely behind schedule!

I clawed down the ladder and practically landed right on top of Aunt Eloise, who had suddenly materialized at the bottom.

"There you are, Georgie!" Aunt Eloise peered up to the loft window. "My goodness, it has to be almost lunch time, already. How do you youngsters get anything done when you waste half of the day?" She started tottering in the direction of the milking stanchions.

I hesitated, one paw in the air, wanting to make a run for the door but knowing, sure as shooting, that my aunt would be hollering at me just as soon as she saw her milk bowl was empty. And this time, I deserved it.

"Uh, Aunt Eloise," I said, trying to pull her attention away from the empty bowl. "Maybe you should start the morning patrol in the loft."

"Nothing doing," she retorted. "Haven't been up there in months. The ladder's getting steeper every year, and Emma doesn't seem to understand when I complain about it." She turned and eyed me. "That's what you're getting paid for. Go right ahead." She resumed wobbling in the direction of the dish.

"Well then, why don't you check the feed room. Surely there's—"

"Just came from there. Nothing's stirring. That's why I'm in desperate need of my breakfast." She reached the food bowl and looked inside. "Now what…"

"Aunt Eloise," I began.

And at that very moment there was a frenzied howling and barking from right outside the barn door. Those yappers had returned and had picked up my scent!

"What in tarnation?" Aunt Eloise said, turning toward the door. She began tottering toward it.

"No!" I said, stepping forward to block her path. "Aunt Eloise, stay away from that door. There are two gigantic dogs out there who are eager to get their jaws into you, and if they did, they'd have you torn to bits in nothing flat."

Aunt Eloise paused and squinted up at me. "I see you've already met."

"Yeah, I guess that's one way of putting it." I sat down next to her, keeping my ears pricked toward the door. "Listen, why don't you let me help you up the ladder. Just in case…well, you know…just in case someone opens the door and the dogs come flying in, you won't be able to…well…uh…they're pretty fast and you're…" I paused.

"Are you saying that I'm too old and dimwitted to take care of myself?" Aunt Eloise's tail swished through the straw behind her.

"No, of course not," I said quickly. "It's just—"

"Did you ever try engaging these 'gigantic' canines in conversation, or did you take a look and run?"

I shook my head. "Conversation isn't what they're after. I could tell the moment I laid eyes on them. These are dangerous beasts, hardened killers, bloodthirsty…"

"Oh, pshaw." She resumed her slow progress to the door. "You took one look and ran, and when a dog sees a cat running, of course he'll chase. It's just his nature." She shook her head. "Poor dumb animals. They can't help themselves."

She'd reached the door, and I could hear the dogs on the other side going wild, baying and clawing at the ground. I threw myself between Aunt Eloise and the widening crack under the barn door.

"Aunt Eloise, you have to listen to me!"

Without warning, a hairy muzzle poked through the crack and a pair of jaws snapped at my leg. I leaped sideways, tail poofed and claws extended, out of reach of the teeth. But then I heard furious growling and more digging sounds outside. Dirt was flying everywhere. I could see paws flashing through the crack, along with an occasional muzzle.

"We need to get up into the loft. Now!" I tried to push her with my head in the direction of the steps, and she toppled onto her side, glaring at me.

"We will not be chased out of our territory by a pair of witless hounds who think they can throw us into a panic with a little snarling and snapping of teeth." She pulled herself with effort to her feet. "If I hadn't trained you myself, I'd be thinking your orange fur is turning a little yellow, young man. We're going to do what we've always done: stand and fight. We come from a long line of fighters."

"Yes, but even the bravest of cats will retreat in order to stay alive to fight another day!"

She ignored me and stuck her head close to the widening crack under the door. "Yoo-hoo," she called.

A pair of jaws appeared through the hole behind her, open and ready to snap. Using my lightning quick reflexes, I shoved my aunt out of the way and pounced on the protruding muzzle, clawing at the nose.

Instantly, the jaws pulled back out of sight, and the howling went up several octaves, turning into a series of pained yips. The other muzzle flashed briefly under the door, sniffing, but I slashed that nose with my claws, also. There were another few yips and squeals, the sound of retreating steps, and then silence.

After a few moments of strained listening, I cautiously poked my head under the door and looked around. The farmyard was completely empty. I breathed a sigh of relief and turned to find Aunt Eloise sprawled motionless in the dust near the door.

"Aunt Eloise?" I said, hurriedly shifting toward her. "Aunt Eloise, are you okay?" I gave her a good poke in the side. She didn't stir. I licked her ears. They didn't twitch. "Aunt Eloise?" I tried once more.

There was no response.

I'd not been quick enough after all. Maybe the dog had managed to chomp her before I'd sunk in my claws. Maybe her heart had failed in fright. I slumped to the ground and swallowed hard, my chest tight. My aunt was dead—killed while I'd been on the job. I hadn't been fast enough to protect her. Sure, she'd always been a little annoying and hard of hearing, but she'd also been so patient, taking the time to train me, an inexperienced kitten, when I'd first arrived at the farm.

She'd shown me how to crouch still as stone, without even flicking my tail, when waiting beside a gopher hole. She'd been there, sitting proudly on the feed bags in the shed with her whiskers high, when I'd caught my first mouse. She'd endured my company for days after I'd gotten caught in the crossfire during the skunk invasion of the chicken house. And when she'd finally retired to the barn, she transferred the title of "Chief of Rodent Security" to me.

But what an awful security officer I'd turned out to be! I suddenly had a terrible feeling—one totally foreign to me: doubt. What if I was incapable of doing my job? What if I'd been kidding myself all these years? What if my aunt had paid the price for my inadequacy?

My whiskers drooped to the ground, but my mind whirred furiously, refusing to believe what I was feeling. There had to be another explanation. Security on the farm had been running smoothly until…

…until that new cat had showed up.

I narrowed my eyes. That pipsqueak hadn't lost any time stealing my spot and sending his slobbery bodyguards after me. And he'd been undermining my authority ever since. True, it'd been the canines who'd chased me up a tree, tried to eat me for breakfast, and then frightened my aunt into an early grave. But they'd called Felix 'Boss,' so I knew it was Felix calling the shots. It was Felix who was responsible.

And what was I doing about it? I glanced around in the semi-darkness. I was cowering, that's what I was doing, hiding in the barn like a helpless kitten instead of acting like the seasoned patrol cat I really was. And those intruders thought they had me trapped.

Well, they had another thing coming. After all, this

was *my* farm and I wasn't going to run. I would get that intruder out of my spot if it was the last thing I ever did!

I clawed the ground in front of me and stood to full height, muscles flexed and fangs showing. "Wish me luck, Aunt Eloise," I muttered to myself as I stalked toward the sun-streaked crack under the door.

"What? What was that?" a shrill voice came from behind me.

I jumped a foot in the air and came down (on all four legs, of course) with my hair feeling like it'd been rubbed all over by one of Emma's balloons. "Aunt Eloise," I squeaked, "you're alive. You're really alive!"

"Well, of course I'm alive. What'd you expect? I may be old, but I'm not out of the game yet. Now come on over here and lend me a shoulder. Tarnation. How did I get into this awkward position anyway?"

I stepped tentatively toward her. "But you were just lying there. I thought …"

"Well, there's the problem. You should do more looking and less thinking. If you'da come a little closer, you'da been able to tell I was just taking my morning snooze."

"But—"

"No buts, young fella. Now get over here and help your poor auntie."

I dutifully nudged my aunt to her feet, and she tottered once more in the direction of her milk bowl. "Now what were we discussing? Confound it. My nap wiped everything clean." She poked her nose into her bowl. "Huh. Where did—"

"You don't remember the dogs?" I interrupted.

She cocked her head and swayed it in my direction, almost overbalancing. "Dogs? We haven't had dogs on this farm since the summer of …"

I shoved my shoulder under her rib cage to keep her upright. "You don't remember them digging a hole under the barn door?"

Her eyes strayed over to the door. "Huh," she said finally. "Wouldn't believe you except that they left a whopper of a hole under the door. I musta been snoozing a mite longer than I'd planned. Why'd they run off?"

"Aunt Eloise, they were about ready to have you for a morning snack. I gave them each a claw to the snout, and they decided you weren't such a treat after all."

"Huh," she said again, and by the way she was looking at me, I could tell her thoughts were whirring. She looked down at her food bowl. "Speaking of snacks …"

I suddenly became very interested in the angle of sunlight beaming down from the loft. "Would you look at that? Must be getting pretty late. I have to catch up to Emma in the garden."

"Georgie …"

"Sorry, don't have time. See you … uh … soon." And I scooted under the door.

"Georgie," my aunt shrilled from inside the barn, "you tell those dogs to come back for a visit, you hear? And you be neighborly."

I scowled as I slunk quickly into the tall grass to the side of the barn.

Sure, I'd be neighborly. Neighborly enough to get Emma over to the old house ASAP to take care of this invasion. Aunt Eloise might not think the dogs were dangerous, but I knew better. And I also knew they were still out there.

Crouching with ears pricked forward, I froze.

Nothing.

I waited for what seemed an eternity before I began inching forward, belly to the ground, careful not to disturb the grass. When I'd finally worked my way to the edge of the patch, I poked my nose out from cover and tested the breeze.

The yard was empty and quiet. Dead quiet. I twitched my tail and eyed the tree by the corner of the brick house. If I could make it that far, I'd have an excellent spot to survey the farmyard while waiting for Emma. I made up my mind to run for it.

I shot out of that grass like a squirrel being chased by—well…by me—but wasn't even halfway across the yard when I heard baying from the rear. Festus was barreling straight for me, cutting off my retreat to the barn. And then Brutus appeared, charging at me from where he'd been hidden behind my tree. It was a trap!

I skidded to a stop and quickly scanned the open territory around me. No trees, no grass, no buildings …. Then my eyes lit upon a pile of small, square hay bales sitting on an open pickup bed a few feet away. I didn't question my good fortune. I didn't stop to ask myself why a pickup with a bunch of bales was sitting in the middle of the farmyard. I just ran for it!

The dogs realized where I was heading a split second too late. I made it to the pickup just inches ahead of the brutes, bounding into the back and clawing my way to the top of the pile with them snapping and jumping below. They leaped around the pickup, tearing at the bales and trying their hardest to climb up after me. I skinnied into a tiny crevice between the bales and listened to the din.

The noise must've brought Ted out of the machine shed. I could suddenly hear him shouting at the dogs to stop tearing up his bales. About that time, I heard gravel whizzing above me and thumping into the hay. Ted had probably scooped it up from the ground to fling at the dogs, not me, but I hunkered down just the same. I knew all about getting hit by friendly fire. I'd once got in the way of a clod of dirt that Emma had launched at a rabbit who'd had the cheekiness to lunch on the lettuce in her garden.

It wasn't long before I heard a few startled yips and yaps, followed by the sound of scurrying feet and then silence. Evidently the dogs, unlike my aunt, were smart enough to retreat when things got dangerous. But how far had they run? Maybe it would be best for me to stay put for a little longer until I was sure the coast was clear.

It seemed like a good idea until I heard the engine start. With a sudden jerk, I felt myself move. Or rather, I felt the bales move—with me along for the ride. It was then that I realized a stack of hay bales wouldn't just be *sitting* in the farmyard. They would be waiting to be moved somewhere.

And now I was going, too!

Chapter Seven
A Free Meal Deal

I squirmed out of my niche and up to the top of a bale to take a look-see. An old pickup carrying a load of hay goes about turtle speed, so I briefly considered jumping down to safety. But the ground looked pretty far away from where I sat, three hay bales high. Just imagine looking down from a three-story building. Would you want to jump? Me neither. Especially with those big tires down there ready to squash me into a pancake.

So I scrunched back into my hole and curled up to endure the ride.

The pickup was not only slow, it also had some serious bouncing and jouncing issues. Its wheels must've hit every single hole and washboard in the long, gravel lane before finally reaching the highway. It reminded me of the time that one of Emma's nephews—brother to the pink princess gal—had visited the farm. Only instead of tiaras and sparkly dresses, he'd brought along a can of soda pop. It looked harmless enough to me as he'd sat down with it on Emma's lawn. He'd started shaking the thing, jiggling it around until I'd gone nearly cross-eyed trying to keep it in sight.

And then he'd pulled the tab.

I have to admit that I shot pretty near as high as the fizz that spouted out of that can. And getting caught in the cross-fire wasn't exactly a delightful experience, either—although it'd been a surprisingly sweet treat to give myself a bath afterwards.

The point was, being on that load of hay was making me feel like that can of soda pop, shaken up and ready to explode.

When we finally reached the pavement, the ride calmed down somewhat—the only discomforts now being wind whistling through the crevices and bits of hay blowing into my face—and I felt suddenly droopy. My quick reflexes and sharp feline brain had been on alert much too long. I melted into a puddle in my nest of hay and fell asleep.

A sudden jerk interrupted my nap. I'd been

dreaming that I was snoozing in a patch of sunlight on my porch, and here I was stuffed in a scratchy load of feed instead. What a disappointment! I heard the pickup's engine turn off and the door slam shut.

Worming my way to the surface, I watched Ted head over to a nearby brick building. I licked a paw and rubbed it across my face, getting the sleep out of my system before testing the air with my super sensitive feline nostrils. Something wasn't quite right. Instead of the green smell of grass, I sniffed a mixture of gasoline and hot cement.

I surveyed the area. The ground below me was gray and hard, radiating heat. There was an entire row of buildings in front of me, and another row behind me. Then it hit me—this pickup was parked in a town!

Yes, I know what a town looks like. I was born in one, after all. I'd spent my kittenhood with my mother and her human, Emma's sister, Twila, in a town much like this one. The first six weeks of my life had been pretty sheltered. Until the day that Emma had stopped by.

"You didn't tell me you had an orange kitten," she'd said to Twila as soon as she'd seen me. "He's perfect. I've been looking for one to replace George the Third!"

(Did you notice that she said I was "perfect?")

I found out later from Aunt Eloise that Emma always has an orange cat around the farm because she thinks they make the best mousers. So I became George the Fourth in a long, illustrious line of orange patrol cats. Just thinking about the day Emma had chosen me made me want to raise my nose into the air, strut a little, and—

Mmmm. I sniffed. What was that wonderful smell? My stomach growled, reminding me that it'd been ages since the bowl of milk in the barn.

I jumped and clawed my way down the bales of hay, then followed my nose over to a building where the scent of grilled meat was especially strong. Through the glass, I could see people sitting at tables and eating. Food was everywhere! This was heaven. Surely one of those nice people would share with me.

I sat on the hot pavement with my tail curled around me, pretending to be half asleep until I saw someone coming toward the door. As the door opened, I sprang to my feet, zipped between a pair of legs, and slid through the crack just in time. Once inside, I put on my best "hungry but friendly" cat expression and sauntered over to the nearest table. Rubbing and purring, I made myself known to the nearest set of legs. A man's face looked down at me.

"What's this?" His eyebrows shot up. "I didn't know Pete had a cat in here." He turned back to his plate of food and ignored me.

Maybe I hadn't made myself clear. I stood on my hind legs and batted at his elbow as he lifted a fork to his mouth. I must've hit him harder than I'd planned. The fork clattered down and a blob of mashed potatoes fell right into my face.

"Blasted cat!" I heard from above. Then I felt a boot from behind. Of course I couldn't see the boot coming because my eyes were still covered with spuds.

Helped along by the boot, I flew forward and smashed into a wall. Now this was definitely *not* how I'd planned to get a meal, but food in the face is better than none at all. I spared a second to clean the goop out of my eyes with my paw and then licked the paw clean. Mmm, good! Now that I'd had my appetizer, I was ready for the main course.

I surveyed the room a little more closely this time, looking for someone more generous than the potatoes guy. Ah! My eyes lit on one of those tiny, noisy humans— babies, I think they're called. This particular one had been placed in a chair taller than everyone else's and was being given pieces of meat by a human sitting nearby. When the large human turned, some of the meat would go into the baby's mouth and some would land on the floor. A spread of free food was just waiting for the taking!

I ambled over and thoroughly cleaned up the area under the tall chair. I figured I was definitely doing someone a favor, too. Now the floor wouldn't have to be scrubbed. Then I sat down beside the chair and waited for more food to rain down. What a life. Maybe Emma should get one of these little humans, too!

The tiny tyke looked down and saw me. His eyes opened wide and he waved his hands around excitedly. He reached down to me with a gooey hand, and—well, I just did what any respectable cat would do. I licked the food off his fingers.

The kid giggled and gurgled some things that sounded like words, but it beats me what he said. Then he turned in his chair and stretched out the other hand. Hey, no problem. If cleaning was what he wanted, I was more than happy to help.

I was in the process of washing off the other set of fingers when the big human noticed him leaning down.

"Tyler, what are you doing?" she said, trying to set him upright again. Then she looked down and saw me in mid lick.

I guess I expected some thanks. After all, I'd mopped the floor and done a terrific job cleaning the kid. His face was still a little dirty, but, hey, I just couldn't reach that far. The lady didn't thank me though. No, siree. Instead she made a horrible scene. She stood up and started shouting for the manager, snatching the kid away so fast that he knocked his knees against the table and started to howl. The other people around me turned and stared. Some pointed and laughed, and one lunged toward me.

I puffed my tail and headed for the door, but of course it was closed. I was trapped inside a room with a mob of hostile humans who were staring and yelling at me.

A tall, red-faced human stumped toward me with a broom in his hands. His face flushed even redder when I ducked under a table. But what did he expect? I wasn't going to sit around and wait for him to pound me!

I dashed from one table to the next with people standing up and scooting chairs out of the way, trying to grab me. Another little human began firing peas and rolls at me. She had amazing accuracy. Too bad I couldn't stick around to clean up the mess.

The noise in the room was deafening, and I was in extreme danger of being grabbed by some angry giant when the door was suddenly opened by an incoming human. I streaked toward the rapidly closing exit like my life depended on it. My head flew through the narrowing gap and most of my body followed. But the door thunked shut right on my fuzzy orange tail.

That brought me to an abrupt, painful halt. I must have been quite a sight, clawing at the cement, yowling and pulling with all my might until, hair by hair, I tugged my tail out of its trap. Then I skedaddled out of that place as fast as my tootsies would take me, thrashing my poor throbbing tip of a tail behind me.

Chapter Eight
Admirers

What a day! First pursued by ferocious, cat-eating dogs and then chased by equally ferocious, cat-hating humans. I galloped along the street, preparing to spring back into the hay bales—until I realized they were gone. Ted had driven off without me!

With loud voices behind me and the empty parking spot in front of me, I have to admit I panicked. I took off at a dead run, turning down this street and that, until I finally ran out of breath and had to stop. Feeling extremely hot and excessively poofed, I sat and licked my fur, bringing it back under control, and then looked around. The sidewalk stretched out in front of me with grass and houses laid out alongside. Absolutely nothing looked familiar.

Where was I? How could I find my way home? I

began padding down the sidewalk, this time paying more attention to the landscape. But the first street looked just like the next—and the next and the next.

"There's no hope for it, George," I muttered to myself. "You got yourself good and lost. You'll be lucky if you ever get back home."

I kept walking, however, because a good security officer will never accept defeat even if his feet are starting to feel like they have bricks tied to them and his whiskers are getting a little droopy.

Resolutely, I kept scanning the territory, ever on the alert for hostile humans or dogs. Then all of a sudden my razor-sharp senses started giving me little snappy signals like the ones they give me when I see mouse tracks in the dust in the garage or when I smell hair on Emma's pant leg that I know isn't mine. My fur felt all tingly, like it was getting ready to poof.

Danger?

I narrowed my eyes and slowed my pace, even more watchful than before, trying to make sense of what I was seeing. There *was* something odd about this street. The cracks on the sidewalk seemed familiar somehow, like a pattern I'd known a long time ago. And that rose bush on my left—where had I seen *it* before?

I came to a stop at the end of the sidewalk. Ahead of me was an empty, grassy lot. Empty, that is, except for a huge cottonwood tree standing at one end. I tilted my head and studied it. There was a peculiar knot on its trunk that looked like a squirrel's face.

Huh. An image flitted through my head, a vague memory of racing up a weathered trunk just like that to catch the squirrel, and then my disappointment when I discovered it was only a hunk of wood.

I just couldn't resist checking it out. I ambled over to the tree and looked around. It seemed to me … It just seemed like there should be a hiding spot around here somewhere. I poked my nose into the overgrown grass by the roots of the tree, and, by golly, there was a kitten-sized hole!

How had I known it would be there? I sat to puzzle this over. Could it be—would it be possible—that this was *my* town? Scratching at my ears with a paw, I tried to remember way back to my kitten days.

If this were my town, I should be able to walk further down the street and find…a certain house. Hmm. A blue house, with a brick sidewalk. And in that house, I should find a human named Twila—Emma's sister, Twila.

Twila could help me get back home!

My ears pricked at the thought, and I immediately jumped up and began trotting down the avenue, eyes straining for that blue house, as excited as if I'd just been offered a full bowl of milk. And there it was!

I bounded across the bricks leading to the front door and was getting ready to yowl a greeting when I heard scratching and scrabbling sounds from the roof above me. I peered upwards, having to blink the sun from my eyes before I could see the black tail that was curling down from the rain gutter. Then there was a flash of a white-mittened paw.

"Oh, bother," said a female voice.

Was it? Could it be ... my mother?

I took a few steps back to get a better view of the roof. A black cat with four elegant white paws was up there, daintily pacing back and forth alongside the gutter, peering down. This cat was definitely not my mother. She was way too pretty.

"Bother *and* blast," the little lady said again, staring at the ground below and obviously not seeing me.

I gave my head a shake to clear the sudden buzz in my brain, then smoothed my fur with a paw and stretched to full height. "Are you in need of assistance?" I called up.

She gave a small jerk. Her ears pricked forward when she saw me. "I don't suppose you'd know an easy way down from this roof?" Then she shook her head. "Of course you don't, being a stranger and all. But I had to ask."

She resumed her pacing.

"You might try the back of the house," I suggested. "There's an ash tree with a limb that's a little too close to the gutter. It doesn't look like it's strong enough to hold a cat, but it will. I guarantee it."

She narrowed her eyes as if she might challenge my suggestion but then turned and scrambled over the roof, disappearing onto the other side. I ambled around the corner of the house and watched as she gingerly put one paw and then another onto the tree limb. It wobbled with her weight but held, as I knew it would.

She clawed her way down the trunk. "Thanks," she said, catching sight of me. "My name is Alice, by the way." She sat on the grass and began to gracefully smooth her fur with her tongue.

I stared, mesmerized by the stylish curve of her white whiskers.

She stopped licking and looked over at me, catching

me in mid stare. "What's yours?"

I flushed, desperately hoping that she couldn't see me turning red underneath my orange fur. "I—uh—my name you mean? I'm, um, George."

"So Um George, how did you know about the limb?" she asked, neatly curling her tail around her feet.

"George. It's just George," I stammered, then tried to casually stretch from shoulders to toes, pulling myself together. "I used to live here. That limb was how I got from roof to ground many times." I paused. "You haven't been here long, have you? You would've figured it out on your own eventually."

She laughed, yawned, and began to lick a paw. "No. I was just let out of the house for the first time today. Twila—you know Twila?"

My ears pricked forward. "Yes, I certainly do."

"Well, I came to live with Twila last week. My first family was moving and couldn't take me with them, and Twila needed another cat to be a companion for the elderly tabby who—"

"My mom," I interrupted, jumping up.

She stopped in mid lick. "What?"

"That elderly tabby is my mom."

"Oh," she laughed. "No wonder. There is a certain resemblance in the shape of your face."

"Uh, yeah." I glanced away, fumbling for something intelligent to say. "The place hasn't changed much."

"Good thing." She nodded toward the peony bush beside the steps. "Your mom's under there right now, fast asleep. Did you come to see her?" She padded over to the bush. "Beatrice. Beatrice, wake up. Guess who's here?"

A pair of green eyes appeared, and then the rest of the rather rotund tabby shuffled out from under the bush. It was Mom.

She shambled closer. "George, is that you?" she said. She leaned forward to peer at me. "It *is* you! Back to visit your old mother! How wonderful!" She began to pad around me, purring so loudly that the vibrations felt like a foot massage through the pavement.

"Hi, Mom," I said awkwardly. She was a lot shorter than I remembered her.

"My goodness, how you've grown. You always used to be so puny. In fact, perhaps you've grown a bit too much." She gave my belly a poke with one paw. "On full feed, are you?"

"Mom, stop it!" I said, glancing at Alice. "I'm not

fat. Those are just my muscles, see?" I arched my back and *stretched* to full height. "You are looking at a finely-tuned, mouse exterminating machine."

"Oh, my," she said, circling me. "When was the last time you bathed?" And she began to lick the mashed potatoes and pea bits that were still stuck to my ears. She may have shrunk, but she was still as bossy as ever.

"Mom, stop it," I complained and tried to squirm out of her reach.

"Hold still," she commanded, licking behind my ears. "You always were a hard one to keep clean."

I could hear Alice giggling next to me. I took a breath to say something, hoping that my brain would come up with a clever retort and wouldn't just leave me there with my mouth hanging open, when the screen door opened and out stepped Twila.

Whew. Saved by the human.

"Who've you got there, Beatrice?" Twila asked as she bent down to pet her. She took a closer look at me. "Why, my goodness. Is that you, George?"

I sat down casually, as if I came for a visit every day.

"Is Emma here, too?" She stepped out into the street and looked back and forth. Then she turned and studied me with a puzzled expression. Suddenly, she scooped me up and hauled me inside. My mom and Alice followed.

Twila put me beside Mom's cat bowl, which happened to be full of the extra-special, expensive food that comes out of a can. At least *she* could understand a cat's feelings. While I helped myself to lunch, Twila picked up the telephone and dialed.

"Emma, this is Twila. How are you today? ... No, actually, I was wondering if you'd seen George lately. ... Not since early this morning? Well, that's incredible. ... No, no that's not what I meant. He's here! ... Well, I have no idea. He must've hiked the five miles into town. ... To visit his mother maybe? ... No really, I'm not pulling your leg. ... Okay, okay. Listen, I'll bring him over later this afternoon when I come for the green beans. ..."

And then the conversation moved on to what Emma was doing in her garden, and how dry it had been, and so on and so on. Boring human stuff. Why talk about the weather when it just *happens*? There's nothing you can do about it anyway.

I preened and stalked around the food bowl looking tough (in between bites, that is) while Twila was telling Emma about my adventures.

Mom was gazing at me with an adoring expression. "My loyal, loving son," she purred every once in awhile, trying to lick my ears again.

Alice's eyes were huge. "Five miles," she finally said. "You walked five miles?"

I turned back to the food bowl and took another bite to avoid answering the question.

"Five miles," she said again, her eyes shining at me. "Wow."

"Yeah, uh," I fumbled, wondering how I was going to get out of this. It's not like I *wanted* to lie, but on the other hand, I'd been running a little short on admiration this week. "Too bad you can't come back to the farm with me," I said, deciding that changing the subject might be best. "For a visit, you know. I could show you all the best places to stalk gophers and uh …"

Alice sat down very close to me, rubbing against my side.

My legs went a little wobbly, and all of a sudden I had to sit down, too. For some reason, being around Alice made me feel a little light-headed. Or maybe that was because of the overly rich food in Mom's bowl.

Just then Twila got off the phone. She got down a box of kitty treats and gave me *two* of them. "You must be starved, George, after a trip like that."

GEORGE AND THE STOLEN SUNNY SPOT

I pulled myself away from Alice and rubbed Twila's legs, attempting an expression somewhere between extreme hunger and muscular power. I was enjoying this. More treats. Appreciative company. Maybe I didn't want to return to the farm after all.

On the other hand, it was my responsibility to take care of that impertinent porch thief at home. If I stayed away too long, he might set his sights on commandeering even more territory—like the garden, or the barn. The choice was clear. No matter how much I might wish to stay, duty was calling me to return. I would just have to enjoy the little time I had before Twila took me home.

I crunched my way through one of the kitty treats and then began nibbling at the other one. My belly was already feeling a little stretched, but I couldn't let a good snack go to waste. It didn't help that my eyelids were beginning to droop. And Alice's voice seemed to be coming from further and further away.

A short snooze is what I need, I decided. Just long enough to clear the cobwebs from my head so I can enjoy Alice's company before I have to go home. Forty winks and no more.

So I curled up on the soft rug by the food bowl and fell asleep.

Chapter Nine
A Hero Returns Home

"Come on, George. Time to go home."

Alice nudged me, and I jumped. Where was I? I rubbed a paw over my eyes. The kitchen—and Alice—came into focus.

"Nice snooze?" she asked.

I changed the eye-rubbing to a paw-licking and tried to look nonchalant. "Just a cat nap."

She grinned. "Pretty long nap. It's late afternoon already."

"What?"

"Come on, George," called Twila, standing at the open front door.

Rats! How had the time gotten away from me? Now I couldn't visit with Alice. I stretched onto my tippy-toes and yawned away the last of the brain fog. Duty was a real pain sometimes. Maybe I should stay here after all.

Alice nudged me again.

"What?" I said. "Are you trying to get rid of me?"

"No silly." She began prodding me toward the door. "I'm going along."

"But how will you …" I began, picturing the rumpus that would ensue if *I* jumped uninvited into the car with Emma.

"I can be very purr-suasive." Alice grinned. "Watch this." She padded over to Twila and began doing figure 8's around her legs.

"What's the matter, Alice?" Twila looked down. "You want to go, too?"

Alice turned on her motor and cocked her head, her blue eyes practically melting as she looked up at Twila.

Twila bent down and rubbed Alice between the ears. "You lovey-dovey. Sure, you can go, too. Why not?"

Now it was my turn for huge eyes. Alice was slick, all right. Maybe I'd have to get some pointers from her on communicating with humans.

I said good-bye to Mom, enduring one more ear-washing in farewell, then followed Alice and Twila out to the car. Alice and I hopped into the front seat as soon as Twila opened the door. I put my front feet up on the dusty dashboard to get a better view of the scenery, and Alice put her feet next to mine. She stood there, swaying gently beside me as the car moved down the street. *My* legs had more of a wobble than a sway, but I told myself it was because I wasn't used to riding in a car.

I soon forgot the wobble, though, as I looked out the windshield. The fence posts were whipping by so fast that I could hardly keep track of them all—and there was no wind. No dust, no bits of hay blasting me in the face. I ducked as a couple of bugs came flying at us and winced as they smacked against the windshield, ending up as a sticky mess on the glass. What a waste of a perfectly good snack.

Way too soon, the car rolled into the farmyard, and Twila parked it under the old cottonwood tree by the garage. Emma came out of the house to meet us and shook her head as I paraded out of the vehicle with Alice on my heels.

"You never know what that cat will do next," she said.

"And he's still in one piece," Twila agreed, as if I'd gone through a battle.

I tilted my nose in the air—just a bit—and said to Alice, "Let's go for a little walk." And I knew where I wanted to walk. Straight past the old house. I had a lady for company, while Felix only had two idiot dogs.

I heard Emma and Twila crunching through the gravel behind us. "How are the new neighbors?" Twila was asking.

"Working out just fine," said Emma. "Everybody's happy with the arrangement."

I laid back my ears. Not *everybody*.

Emma ignored my obvious disagreement and continued. "I'm happy that the old house is being taken care of, Ted's happy that he has some extra help now, Jason's happy to be back in his home territory, and Lil's happy because—well, newlyweds are always happy."

Emma and Twila both laughed.

"Jason's parents live in town, right?" Twila asked.

Emma nodded.

"Then I'd imagine they're happy, too, now that their son and daughter-in-law are living so close."

I gave a disgusted sneeze.

Alice looked over at me. "Allergies?" she asked.

"Yeah," I replied. "To an overabundance of happiness."

Emma and Twila had stopped at the gate. Lil was sitting on the porch with Felix in her lap. When she caught sight of us, she put Felix down and came over to the fence.

I kept my eye on Felix. As soon as his feet touched the ground, he padded over to *my* puddle of sun and curled up there, twitching his whiskers at me.

"Hi, Lil," said Emma. "Thought you might like to meet my sister, Twila. She lives in town. She's on an errand of mercy today, bringing George back to us."

"Nice to meet you," said Twila.

"Nice to meet you, too," Lil echoed. "Bringing George back from where?"

Twila shrugged. "Strangest thing. George evidently walked the five miles into town. I found him on my doorstep this afternoon."

"Five miles? You're kidding!" She wrinkled her forehead and studied me.

I sat on my haunches and straightened to full height in my best 'iron cat' pose.

Emma glanced down at me. "Well, I've heard of cats that could do it, but I never guessed my George would. I should have known he could, though. He certainly has enough smarts to make it safely."

"What a guy," said Alice from beside me.

None of the humans could understand her, of course, but I noticed that Felix's whiskers went rigid.

Lil frowned. "I don't want George to give Felix any ideas. He's never been past the house. He'd probably get lost in the lawn."

Emma smiled. "I'm sure Felix won't wander off. George is just a special kind of cat. The orange ones always are."

By now my head was so swelled, it was about ready to burst. I threw a condescending look over in Felix's direction. His ears were flattened against his head, and he wasn't smiling anymore.

So there, Felix, I thought. Now you understand why *I'm* in charge.

I figured by this time, Felix would be ready to bow to authority and hand back my spot. All I would have to do was make a visit that evening and graciously accept his surrender.

Chapter Ten
Confrontations

I spent the rest of the afternoon showing Alice around the place. We had a great time climbing trees. Then I showed her how to stalk mice behind the barn, and we both bounded around in the grass, tails held high, when she actually caught one.

We ended the visit by wandering over to join Emma and Twila in the garden while they were picking green beans. I showed Alice some grasshopper pouncing techniques, and when we'd both caught several, we sat in the shade under the rhubarb leaves and talked.

Much too soon, Twila scooped her up. Alice looked down at me with a smile that started my legs wobbling again.

"I'll be back," she called, as Twila carried her away.

Wow. I felt like I could stay in the garden forever,

basking in the warmth of the day's events. But soon I found I was basking in more sunshine than I cared for. My whiskers were even droopy from the heat. If I'd been on my porch in my spot, I could've just rolled from the puddle of sunshine into the shady corner. I wouldn't have even needed to wake up completely to do it.

Too bad the spot was still unavailable. But that would change very soon. I'd have a bite of supper and then head over to the old house to take Felix's full surrender.

I put my tail straight up in the air and padded regally over to the garage, practicing my victory march for the grand occasion. As I was helping myself to my full food bowl (just dry kibbles, of course), I heard Emma go into the house.

Everything was peaceful outside. No tractor engines, no wind scraping branches across the roof, no birds singing …

No birds. That was strange.

I pricked my ears. It was *too* quiet.

Suddenly, Brutus and Festus burst through the door, baying and howling, fangs showing, coming straight for me. Instantly, I poofed my fur and made a flying leap for the rear bumper of the pickup parked next to me. The metal was slick and I almost overshot my mark, but I managed to dig my claws into the rubberized tread on the back, and with another leap, I shot into the box and up to the top of the cab. I would be safe here for a few moments, at least. I didn't know if those bruisers made a practice of jumping into the back of a pickup for rides through the pasture or not. If they knew how to do it, I was a goner.

They were circling around, trying to find enough room to spring into the box, when I heard a shout from outside. Emma came flying through the garage door brandishing a long spoon from her kitchen. "You dogs get out of here," she shouted. "Get! Get!"

She gave them a couple of solid whacks as they tried to squeeze past her to get out of the door. I heard her chase them all the way back to their yard and clunk the gate shut. Then there was silence again. I was pretty sure she had locked the gate. But on the other hand, I'd been pretty sure the gate was locked when I'd wandered back from the garden.

I wondered if those dogs could open gates. My eyes narrowed. If they could get loose on their own, I was in real trouble. Felix could send them after me at any time. I wasn't even safe in my own garage!

I also realized that if Felix was sending out the cavalry to attack me in my home territory, he certainly wasn't considering surrender. This was definitely an act of war.

I did my evening rounds very cautiously, keeping an eye on that locked gate the entire time and hoping that Lil and Jason would pack up their animals and leave as they had yesterday. No such luck. The house lights went on, Lil carried Felix into the house, the big bruisers bedded down on the porch, and the pickup and trailer remained firmly parked in place. All unfavorable signs that led me to believe that the old house was now permanently occupied.

No wonder I was a little cranky when Pauline gave me her evening report. It didn't help that the slant of her nose was clearly more severe than normal when I told her that the gophers in the pasture were just going to have to wait. Now that those trespassers were posing as legal residents, I had to keep them under constant surveillance.

Then I bedded down for the night in the barn instead of my usual spot in the garage. Aunt Eloise was naturally suspicious of why I was there, but I told her that I was going to spend the night on patrol in the loft. That seemed to satisfy her. I'd never have heard the end of it if I'd admitted I was there to get out of reach of the dogs.

The next morning I was sitting in my tree, wondering when it would be safe to go on mouse patrol again, when Emma walked by on her way to the garden. She must've noticed me sitting up there, staring at the dogs basking in the sun. And she must've noticed that those two bruisers weren't enjoying a sunny spot in their own yard but were instead sprawled in the soft sand of the driveway, a few feet from the base of my tree.

The gate, of course, was open again.

Her mouth set in a firm line, and she marched up the walk and knocked on the door.

It's about time she noticed something's wrong, I thought, stretching to get a better view.

Lil came to the door. "Hi, Emma."

Emma nodded. "Hi, Lil. How are things going?"

"Just fine. And you?"

"Well, I have a little problem and maybe you can help. I was hoping you could keep the gate shut so your dogs wouldn't get out."

"Oh." Lil stepped out onto the porch and looked toward the gate, frowning. "I thought it *was* shut."

Emma shrugged. "Maybe Jason forgot to latch it when he left this morning. I'd appreciate if you could keep an eye on it, though. Last night, your dogs were out terrorizing George in my garage, and who knows when they'll decide to get into the corrals and go after the sheep."

Lil hesitated then nodded. "Sure. No problem."

"Thanks," Emma said, and turned down the steps.

Lil called from the steps, "Come here, Festus. Here, Brutus."

The dogs stretched and glanced up into the tree at me. I resisted the impulse to sneer. That would be very unprofessional, after all. Instead, I clawed my way down the trunk and held up my tail like a flag to parade after Emma to the garden. But I risked one small glance behind me.

Felix chose just that moment to magically materialize on the porch. It seemed as if he'd simply sauntered out of the house through the wall next to the screen door, but I knew that walking through walls was impossible. He must've been curled up next to the door, hidden so that I hadn't seen him. The pipsqueak looked at the dogs, who were now slumping up the sidewalk, and then at Lil, who was shutting the gate.

I turned my eyes back to the garden, however, before he could see me watching him.

Lil's voice carried very clearly as she walked back up the sidewalk. "Felix-kitty, we'll have to keep an eye on the dogs now. I don't know how in the world they're getting out, but I guess they're causing trouble with that *other* cat."

I imagined the kid standing there with his black, glittering eyes pointed directly at me. I could almost feel the hole they were burning in my back. But I didn't give him the satisfaction of turning around. The dog situation, at least, was under control.

Chapter Eleven
Framed

The next few days were absolutely wonderful. Emma told anyone who stopped by about my mysterious trip to town, and there were "oohs" and "ahs" and kitty treats galore. To make it even nicer, the old gate had a brand new lock on it. Now I could stroll by at leisure—which was whenever I saw Felix out on the porch, of course. The dogs would go wild, and Felix would flatten his ears at me, but there was nothing he could do about it.

On the other hand, there was nothing I could do about my sunny spot, either. I still hadn't thought of a way to get Felix out of the yard and away from his bodyguards.

My newfound peace came rapidly to an end, however. One morning, about a week after my trip to town, I was in the garage having lunch after a morning on patrol. Suddenly Emma came stomping in the door.

"G-e-o-r-g-e!" she hollered.

Uh, oh, I thought. *What did I do now?*

She spotted me as I slunk into the back corner of the garage. "You bad, bad, *bad* cat," she yelled. "I work all summer getting my coleus patch to look just perfect, and you roll around in it like it was your personal playground! Now the plants are all twisted and broken off. They're ruined!"

She grabbed the handle to the door that she always leaves open for me. "You can just sit in here and think about how to behave!" The door slammed shut behind her with such force that I could feel the building shudder.

I peeled myself off the wall where I'd been plastered during her tirade, then sat and puzzled over her words. I *had* been sleeping in the flowers this morning, but only in the marigolds. They're wild and bushy as weeds, and Emma never notices me curled up in there.

So if it wasn't me who mangled her plants then who was it?

It took me all of three seconds to hit upon a suspect.

That little sneak, Felix, I thought. *I'll bet he figured out a way to squash the greenery just to get me into trouble.*

Well! I had some investigating to do, and pity the poor cat if he proved to be the culprit!

Emma let me out of the garage as the sun was sinking behind the trees. I'd snoozed for most of the day so I would be ready for some late night investigating.

I watched the neighbors' yard from behind my tree, hoping that the dogs would soon go into the house for the night. But no such luck. They seemed content to sleep under the open stars smack dab in the middle of the yard. It was evident that I would have to draw upon my superior spying abilities to sneak past those yappers.

I decided that the back yard would be a good place to start. The trees behind the old house hadn't been trimmed in years. They were so overgrown that I was sure I could climb a branch *outside* the fence, make a flying leap, and land on a branch *inside* the fence. If I did it just right, I might be able to reach the house without even touching the ground.

How hard could it be? I thought. I'd seen squirrels do it all the time, especially when I thought I'd finally cornered one.

It didn't take me long to find a tree with branches

that drooped well into the yard. I eased my way out onto one of the thicker limbs and gauged the distance to the neighboring tree. The gap between the branches looked wider than I'd figured.

Hmm. This might get tricky.

I crouched down on the branch and bunched up my muscles, ready for the spring. Unfortunately, crouching caused the limb to swing gently downward, and when I launched into the air, the branch sprang back up with enough force to give me an extra shove that I hadn't planned on. I suddenly found myself in midair—and way off course. This flying business wasn't as easy as the squirrels made it look!

I twisted my body to avoid a face full of leaves as I swung toward the tree and landed—whump—against the trunk. It all happened so quickly that I couldn't manage to catch hold of the bark with my claws before sliding down to the ground. At least I landed at the bottom on all four feet.

It took me a second to catch my breath. This was ridiculous. I could've just climbed the fence and strolled across the yard. It would have been easier and much less painful.

Suddenly I heard the patter of feet rounding the

corner. I scrabbled quickly to the top of the tree and flattened myself into a bushy clump of leaves. Just in time. Through the curtain of leaves, I could see Brutus approaching. He cocked his head to the side as if listening. Then he shook his ears and trotted closer, nose to the ground, sniffing his way over to the fence and back again. Now I was glad that I had "flown" over the fence. I hadn't left my scent in a telltale path across the grass.

Brutus stopped, scratched an ear with his hind foot, and looked around once more. "Huh. I could've sworn I heard something back here," he said as he padded away.

I sighed in relief and surveyed the territory. By crossing a few branches, I could get right up next to the house. My plan was to crawl over the roof of the house and onto the wooden awning that covered the porch.

I climbed onto a likely-looking limb that began to bend alarmingly under my weight. Maybe I *do* need to go on a diet, I thought uneasily. But then it occurred to me that I could use the "bounce" trick I'd just learned to propel myself onto the roof. I crouched down, then up, down, then up, with the branch dipping more deeply each time. When I was at an even level with the roof on the upswing, I was ready. With all the grace I could muster, I disengaged from the branch and flew over to the roof, landing with a distinct "thunk."

I froze for a moment, listening, but no canine showed his snout. They'd probably gone back to sleep. At least I could hope. I crept up the roof, slunk onto the awning and looked over the edge, flattening myself as much as possible against the shingles.

From there I could see the dogs napping. However, I couldn't spy Felix anywhere. "Probably put inside for the night," I muttered to myself. "That kid is nothing but a pansy."

The thought of pansies turned my mind to the matter at hand—flowers. I carefully clawed my way down one of the support columns and landed noiselessly on the porch. Keeping one eye on the snoozing hounds, I crept around the porch and inspected all of the familiar nooks and crannies. One of the dogs twitched his nose and gave a sigh. I immediately tensed, ready for retreat. But there was no further movement.

I padded over to the food bowls next to the door.

Everything looked normal. I was frustrated. All this work for nothing!

I sat down next to the bowls, still keeping an ear turned toward the dogs. What should I do now? I glanced into the bowls. They weren't full, but there were still a few pieces in the bottom of each one. I licked my lips. Surely I'd be able to think better after a snack.

Ever so quietly, I crunched the remaining kibbles. Delicious. Definitely better than the farm store variety that Emma buys. Kinda like when Emma's niece was here and she had a choice between a cookie or a carrot for a snack, she'd always choose the cookie. Felix's food was definitely the cookie rather than the carrot.

As I leaned over to lick the last of the crumbs, something caught my eye. There, trapped between the bowl and the house, was a stray leaf of coleus. My eyes widened. Felix *had* been involved in squashing the greenery.

My claws unsheathed just at the thought of it. I would love to get my paws on that pipsqueak and teach him a lesson or two. Too bad it wasn't possible to walk through walls.

Hmmm.

I padded over to the door, peering and poking and sniffing but couldn't find anything unusual. Guess that proved my point. My eyes had just been playing tricks on me when they'd seen Felix appear on the porch, seemingly out of nowhere. It was hard to imagine where he'd been hiding, though. The floorboards were swept perfectly clean. Not the usual mounds of leaves or twigs to provide cover.

My nose twitched. The normal scent of moldery leaves had been replaced with an extra strong smell of fresh paint. My nose twitched again. I put a paw over my face to hold back the tickle from the fumes, but it didn't work.

Aaa-shtoo! The sneeze blew out of me with enough force to send me backward a couple of steps. I bumped up against the door …

… and froze.

Two hairy heads popped up from the grass. Four glittery eyes trained on me. There was a split second of deadly silence before the air was shattered with a cacophony of woofing and baying.

I must admit that I added to the din with a little yowling of my own before my super-fast reflexes kicked into overdrive. I dove for the edge of the porch, but Brutus had anticipated my move and was waiting for me at the bottom. I tried to skitter to the other edge, but Festus had already bounded up the steps to cut me off.

I backed away from the snarling beast, puffed and ready with my claws. By that time, Brutus had joined his cohort on the porch, and they were both growling and snapping their teeth. I retreated, slinking backwards until my rear end hit the wall.

Great. Nowhere left to go.

The pair of bruisers seemed to sense that I was out of options. They crouched, gathering themselves for the final spring. I shifted against the wall, turning to face them full on, unsheathing my claws, ready to face death fully armed—when the wall gave way behind me.

I felt a sudden draft on my backside, and my legs scrabbled and scratched at a slick surface that was definitely not part of the floorboards on the porch. I risked a glance behind my shoulder and was horrified. My hind end had completely disappeared from view. If I'd had a choice, I would have jumped forward to make sure it was still attached, but I was between a rock and a hard spot, so to say.

Hmmm. More accurately, I was between some very visible snapping teeth and a very mysterious, invisible drafty spot. The drafty spot seemed less painful.

I pulled myself backward, further into the draft and away from the dogs. They noticed immediately that I was disappearing and rushed for me, drool flying. But it was too late. I'd already yanked my head through the strange opening, shutting out all sight of the porch and the dogs and flinging myself into the unknown darkness.

Chapter Twelve
Trapped

I scrabbled around on the slick surface, totally off balance until I thwacked against a tall, hard, box-like object at one end of the room. Finally, with the giant box holding me upright, I was able to regain my balance. Whew! My muscles went limp with relief. I was safe.

Just then, my sensitive whiskers picked up vibrations coming from right beside me. The box I was leaning against—was purring!

My fur poofed and I leaped backwards, claws instantly unsheathed for battle. I'm not usually this jumpy around strangers, but since I was inside Felix's house, I had to assume that this critter was hired to guard Felix as he slept, same as those canines who were still raising a ruckus outside. I peered at the enemy with my extra sharp, darkness defying eyesight, ready to spring if it made any fast moves.

But it just sat there.

I crept closer and batted at it with my claws, then immediately sprang out of range to avoid a possible counter-attack. The beast's smooth, armor-like surface easily repelled the scratch, but it still didn't move.

Once again, I slipped closer and listened. Straining to hear over the din of barking dogs outside, I could just make out a faint hum coming from inside of it. I batted at it again. It didn't feel alive. It felt cold and solid like … Hmm.

A refrigerator.

From the depths of my memories, I pulled up an image of Twila opening a refrigerator like that in her kitchen. She'd kept milk for us kittens inside. Quickly I glanced around, noticing other kitchen similarities. The pipe called a sink that spouted water; the high, flat surfaces called counters that cats were not allowed to walk on; the big box called a stove that got so hot, it would burn your paws if you stood on it. Yep. This was definitely a kitchen. I'd accidentally succeeded in entering the old house.

But now was hardly the time to be invading enemy

territory. The dogs were barking and howling loud enough to outdo an entire pack of coyotes, and Felix's humans were sure to come running to find out what all the ruckus was about.

My fur shivered and threatened to poof. I had no idea how I'd gotten into the house and even less of a notion how to get out. Then a light blinked on from somewhere in the distance, and I heard footsteps above me.

Looking around quickly, I could tell there were no good hiding spots in the kitchen. There was an open doorway to the side of me, and although the light got brighter in that direction, it surely would be safer to go that way than to stay where I was and be caught in plain sight. I dashed through the opening and found myself in a larger room that was bare except for some big, stuffed chairs scattered here and there.

A living room. Twila had a room like this, too. But I didn't have time to look around and compare this place to hers. The footsteps were coming closer, starting down a set of stairs that I could see just ahead of me. I hugged the edges of the walls, desperate to find some corner in which to take cover.

Then I spotted a particularly large chair—a couch,

I think it's called—sitting against the far wall. I leaped across the room and dove behind it, the loud thumping of my heart almost drowning out the sound of the feet coming down the stairs. Carefully, I peeked out from my hiding spot and watched as Jason came into view. His mouth was set in a straight line as he strode across the room.

"Blasted dogs," he muttered. "Gonna wake up the entire farm."

I heard the kitchen door squeak open and his footsteps stomp outside. There was some muffled shouting, a few more barks and whines and then silence. It seemed like an eternity before the kitchen door opened again.

"What's wrong?" Lil's voice called from the top of the stairs.

Jason's footsteps tromped across the living room and up the steps. "The dogs probably saw some critter outside the yard and went crazy. They've calmed down now."

More footsteps. Then the light went out and it got quiet. Very, very quiet.

For several moments, I remained crouched there in the darkness debating what I should do next. Now that

I was in the house and the dogs weren't, I'd love to get my paws on that rude little conniver of a cat. But if I found Felix, he'd likely yowl until the humans came running, and then there'd be a terrible rumpus.

Nope. I simply couldn't let myself get caught in enemy territory. The best time for reconnaissance would be when Felix was home but the humans weren't. What I needed to do now was figure out how I'd mysteriously stumbled into the house in the first place, then I could leave and come back at a more opportune time.

I crawled out from behind the couch and listened intently. The refrigerator was still humming softly, and somewhere a cricket was tuning his wings. I began my silent retreat across the living room and into the kitchen and had almost reached the place where I'd first stumbled inside when some small *whuff* of air caught my attention.

Instantly, I dropped into a crouch and swiveled my ears, straining them forward until they detected an ever so slight catch in breath, a barely audible snuffling, the merest whisper of a whine … all of those faint sounds coming from the region of the screen door. And then I realized—the dogs were waiting for me right outside the door. They had me trapped!

Or at least trapped for the moment. I frowned as I thought. From my surveillance of the place, I knew that Jason left for work early in the morning. I'd also observed that the dogs followed him over to the garage when he came out of the house. Maybe I could sneak out while he was distracting them. That, of course, depended on whether Lil or Felix were in the kitchen at the time, but I didn't have any better ideas at the moment. If necessary, I'd think up a Plan B in the morning.

I took another look around. So where should I take cover for the night? I peered across the kitchen, deep in thought. My eyes fastened on something lying under the counter. Was that what I thought it was? I shook my head and blinked, but the object stayed right there. Cautiously I crept across the cool, slick floor to investigate.

My eyes hadn't deceived me. There, tucked away under the counter, was another cat bowl. Felix had two bowls—an inside bowl and an outside bowl—all to himself. *Two bowls.* That pipsqueak was so spoiled, it's a wonder he hadn't collapsed into a rotten heap by now. And this bowl was almost full. But I suppose I shouldn't be surprised. After all, how much can one puny cat consume?

Even so, I couldn't believe that Felix had left this food lying about. This was the extra, extra special kind. The soft, chunky stuff that comes in a can. For you humans out there, think chocolate fudge cake. (Emma has often said that she would do *anything* for chocolate fudge cake.)

My nose twitched at the heavenly aroma. It wasn't my food, but ...

But those weren't Felix's coleus plants that he'd so thoughtfully smashed, either. Too bad for you, Felix, I thought. You should've finished your supper while you had a chance. I put my nose in the bowl and had most of it chowed down before I stopped.

What would Felix do when he discovered his supper was gone? Would he alert the rest of the household? Would I be found? I looked regretfully at the remainder in the bottom of the bowl. I'd better leave those last couple of bites. The kid might just suppose that he'd eaten more supper than he remembered. What with the kibbles I'd eaten out on the porch, I was feeling pretty full anyway.

I stretched and yawned, feeling full *and* sleepy.

Maybe I shouldn't have eaten so much of that rich food. No, I could handle it. All I needed was a hidden corner where I could tuck myself away for the rest of the night.

I wandered back toward the living room. Behind the couch had been a perfect spot. A bit of a tight fit but definitely out of sight. As I crossed from the slippery kitchen floor onto the carpet, my toes curled into the thick plush. Imagine—Felix had something like this to sleep on every night. And he was still nowhere to be seen. I wondered how his bed could be more comfy than this.

Unfortunately, wading through the thick stuff was becoming a little difficult. I was having trouble lifting my paws high enough. My head was getting heavy, too. I yawned again. It was such a long way back to where the couch sat against the wall.

I looked around. There was a smaller chair only a few steps away. True, it was in plain sight—practically in the middle of the room—but it was draped with a large, fringed blanket. How handy. I wouldn't need to go all the way over to the couch. I could crawl under the blanket and be hidden just fine. My legs felt so heavy that I didn't know if I'd be able to make it that far, but my super-tuned muscles managed the distance.

The blanket had been tucked in around the cushion of the chair. It took me a bit of pawing and clawing to loosen the edges and crawl underneath. All of that effort exhausted me, and I barely got myself curled and hidden away before I fell asleep. Fast asleep.

Chapter Thirteen
Captured and Convicted

I was in the middle of a very pleasant dream, chasing Felix through the hills in our pasture with no dogs in sight, when I suddenly heard a loud scream. At first I thought it was Felix screaming, which might explain why I didn't open my eyes quickly enough to escape. As a result, I was still traveling back from dreamland when the blanket was thrown off of me and I was hauled up by the scruff of my neck.

I quickly shook the last of the sleep fog out of my brain and blinked at the sunlight peeking through the windows. Good grief—I'd overslept! I twisted in midair to get a good look at my assailant.

It was Lil. And she was not happy. "Just *look* at what you've done to my afghan, you awful cat! My grandma knitted it special for me and ... and I could just ...

just…" At that point, she couldn't seem to think of what to say. Her face turned red, and she shook me so hard I could hear my brains rattle. "Just *look*!" she said again, as if I didn't hear the first time.

And so I looked. But I couldn't figure out what the problem was. It still looked like a blanket. True, it was no longer tucked into the cushion, and there seemed to be a few more threads sticking out here and there. But overall, it was still a blanket.

"You've ruined it, you mangy cat. Just *ruined* it!" she said, tightening her grip on the back of my neck and lugging me through the room—none too gently, I might add.

As she carried me to the kitchen door, I noticed Felix sitting next to his food bowl with a smirk on his face. I'd just bet that he put Lil up to this. I wanted to give him a good swipe with my paw, but Lil had me through the screen door before I could attempt to wiggle free.

She marched me over to Emma's house double-quick and pounded on the door. The minute Emma stepped out, Lil burst into her tale of woe. "Emma, this cat … this *troublemaker* cat, snuck into my house overnight and tore up the living room…"

What! I hadn't touched anything except the silly blanket!

"… and my poor Felix is starving to death because this *troublemaker* gobbled all the food right out of Felix's dish in the kitchen…"

Now wait a minute! No cat could possibly starve to death with all that fancy food lying about.

"… and I know this *troublemaker*, George, is terrorizing my animals because my sweet little Felix won't even step foot off the porch, and the dogs bark and whine whenever the big bully comes around…"

Sure they bark. It's part of their "turn the cat into mincemeat" routine. Surely she doesn't need a translation from doggy dialect to understand *that*.

"And I don't know how to keep my animals safe anymore with this troublemaker sneaking into our house. And … And …"

And then she burst into tears.

I was still dangling from Lil's hand, getting soaked by her blubbering, and thinking that I couldn't believe my ears. She thought *I* was terrorizing *Felix*? That rotten cat … that conniver … that sneaky, underhanded—*beast*. How had he managed to look so pitiful that *I* became the bad guy? My claws instantly unsheathed, and I took a couple of swipes at the image of Felix's smirking face that had materialized in front of me. Unfortunately, Felix was nowhere in sight, so Lil took the brunt of my claws.

She yelped and would've dropped me, except that quick-thinking Emma caught me by the scruff of my neck. "George," she said in a voice that curled my toes.

I quickly realized it would be in my best interest to get away until things calmed down a bit. I started to squirm, but her fingers tightened into bands of steel.

"Don't go anywhere," she told Lil. "I'll be right back."

I struggled even harder. But she held me firmly at arm's length while she stomped past the garage and over to the old, empty chicken coop. She unlatched the gate to the dusty pen, dumped me inside, and relocked the exit before I could spring to my feet.

Putting her hands on her hips, she glared at me. "Now I've got to go back over there and calm Lil down before she packs up and takes off with Jason in tow. And *if* I'm successful by the end of the day, I *may* let you out. But it might be to my advantage to ship you back to town and let Felix take up mouse patrol duties around here. At least he doesn't bully the other animals, claw the furniture, and sit on the flowers."

Then she turned and stomped off, leaving me locked up in the poultry pen. Talk about an overreaction.

My whiskers drooped. If it were up to Felix to patrol for mice, the place would be overrun with rodents in a matter of days. But she couldn't see that because Felix had bamboozled her just like he'd done with Lil. I flattened my ears. If she'd only let me out, I'd wallop Felix into the next county, dogs or no dogs. But he was the trusted farm cat now, and I was impounded in a chicken pen. It was the smelliest, most humiliating fate imaginable.

I curled myself into a miserable ball in the corner, trying to disappear. Eventually I fell into a deep sleep and dreamt that I was trapped with a flock of giant, angry chickens who were trying to peck out my eyes.

I didn't think the situation could get any worse.

Little did I know.

Chapter Fourteen
In the Pen

The sun was well past midday when I finally woke up. No use sitting around feeling sorry for myself, I thought, and decided to prowl the corners of the pen looking for an escape route. The problem with chicken pens, though, is that they have special security features designed to keep varmints out. And those same features were likely to keep me *in*. The place had chicken wire on three sides as well as the top, and the gate fitted snugly and latched securely.

The pen was attached to the chicken house on its fourth side. I climbed the ramp, peered through the chicken-sized door, and inspected the darkened interior, but couldn't see a hole anywhere.

Emma came a little later, bringing pans of food and water. I purred and rubbed against the wire, trying to look as sweet and innocent as possible, but she wasn't having any of it. "George, I'm still madder than mad. It was all I could do to sweet-talk Lil into calming down and sticking around, and if she sees you out and about, it might upset her all over again."

She slid the pans through the doorway and left.

I flattened my ears and slouched down in the shade again, resigned to yet more hours of boredom.

Then an old silver Chevy pulled into the yard. Twila's car. I twitched my whiskers and put my chin on my paws. Her arrival was nothing to get excited about. Twila visited Emma all the time.

But when Twila climbed out of the car, she turned and waited for someone else to hop out. Someone with black fur and four white paws. My hair immediately stood on end. Oh, no. Not now! Alice couldn't see me like this!

I looked around frantically for a place to hide, but the entire pen was in full view. That left only one choice. I bolted up the ramp into the old chicken house, trying not to inhale the particles of chicken manure, dust, and feather fluff that floated around me in a cloud.

Hopefully Alice would think that I was out on patrol.

I sat as still as if I were on a rodent stakeout, waiting. And waiting. The silence settled down on top of me like a blanket, along with all the dust and feathers. No matter how hard I tried, I couldn't keep those pervasive particles from infiltrating my nose. When I'd choked back enough sneezes to have easily blasted all the dust from the chicken house, and my muscles were getting stiff enough that I felt nearly as permanently fixed as the nesting boxes in the corner, my curiosity got the best of me. I risked a quick peek through the doorway.

Alice was sitting on the sidewalk in Emma's yard, tail curled around her feet and head cocked to one side. I tried to beam a few thoughts her way. Just find a comfy spot and take a nap, Alice. George is out on mouse patrol and you won't be seeing him today. She finally flicked her tail and scratched her ear as if to say 'Oh, well,' and headed toward the house.

Safe! I thought.

Then she paused and looked over at the old house next door.

Time seemed to stretch and slow as I watched her turn and pad down the sidewalk towards Felix's (and the dogs') abode. "No!" I tried to scream. "Don't do it,

Alice! Those dogs will have you for lunch!" But for some reason, the words got tangled in my throat. As she hopped over the fence, I closed my eyes and held my breath, not able to watch while she was chomped into tiny pieces. I listened for the growling and barking to begin, but there was silence.

Maybe, just maybe, Jason had taken those brutes with him for the afternoon.

I opened my eyes, which did no good. She was already behind the row of cedars that lined the front yard. I waited and waited, hoping for her to reappear. After an endless time, I gave up and slunk over to a smelly nest in the far back corner of the chicken house, huddling there and thinking. She probably just went around to the back yard and through the trees, still looking for me, I told myself.

Yet somehow I knew that wasn't true. The hair on the back of my neck was prickling the way it does when I can sense there's going to be trouble. But there was nothing to do except wait for it to find me.

I must've dozed off. From far away, I thought I heard Alice calling, "George … George …" Then I jerked awake and realized that Alice's voice hadn't been a dream. I could really hear her calling from outside the chicken pen.

"George, it's not going to do you any good to hide. I know you're in there!"

I froze. What was I going to do? I couldn't let her see me like this! Hurriedly, I pushed a paw over my fur. It's hard to project an air of authority when you're covered with chicken feathers and dusty poultry poo.

"George, come on out or I'll never let you hear the end of this!"

I took a deep breath. Guess I had no other choice. Throwing back my shoulders and lifting my tail into the air, I paraded down the ramp as if I were totally in control of the situation.

Then I stopped in my tracks. Alice wasn't alone. She'd brought that little vermin, Felix, with her.

Alice smiled when she saw me. "Hi, George. Felix told me you were here. Didn't you see me get out of the car with Twila? You should've hollered at me, and I would've come over sooner."

"Yeah, well ..." I answered, trying to smile at her and glare at Felix at the same time.

"He was probably embarrassed," Felix cut in.

"Poor George," Alice said, tilting her head with a look of sympathy.

"Poor George," Felix echoed, looking straight at me with what could only be a glow of satisfaction. "Stuck in a pen like a common … chicken."

I narrowed my eyes at him, but forced my ears to stay upright. "That's the kind of comment I'd expect from someone still wet behind the ears," I said, casually lifting a paw to polish my whiskers. "It's all in the line of duty. I've been around long enough to know that humans often jump to conclusions and blame the cat for whatever goes wrong."

Alice sat gracefully on the grass. "Felix told me you'd scratched up Lil's furniture, gobbled his food, and harassed the dogs."

"And that's where jumping to conclusions comes in." This time I didn't attempt to disguise my glare. "The truth is that those dogs trapped me on *my* porch in the middle of a search and rescue mission." I *had* been searching for clues, after all, in an attempt to rescue Emma's plants from any further disaster.

Felix laughed, "Sure …"

"And my only escape was through the … the …"

"The cat door?" Alice helpfully supplied me with the word.

"Yeah, the cat door. And then I was trapped inside the house because the mutts wouldn't give up. I was starving to death by that time, and I didn't figure anyone *neighborly* …" I flicked my tail at Felix, "… would mind if I had a few bites of food. Especially since this *neighbor* has two food bowls all to himself."

Felix opened his mouth again, but I plowed ahead.

"And I needed to hide since I knew the human population in the house wouldn't be happy to see me, so I used the blanket to go undercover, so to say." I looked straight at Felix. "I did *not* claw the furniture. I did *not* harass the dogs. Those are just malicious rumors and misunderstandings being spread by others on this farm."

Alice looked over at Felix.

His ears twitched, but he smiled at her. "Yeah, and who are you going to believe? The cat who's trusted by the humans, or the one who's been sent to the pen?"

"You little fink. I oughta …" I snarled.

"You oughta what, you lousy liar?" he snarled back.

I aimed a claw at him through the wire, but he was standing too far away.

He puffed his fur and hissed.

"Stop it, you two!" Alice stood, her ears flattened

and tail twitching. "I came for a visit hoping for good conversation and a lively mouse hunt, and instead I get a brawl. Next time I'll just stay home!" She turned and marched toward Emma's house.

"Alice, wait." I called after her.

But she kept walking.

Felix started after her. "Don't …" he began. Then he went rigid.

"What's the deal, kid?" I growled. "What are you scared of?"

Felix looked at me with wide eyes, hesitated for one more heartbeat, then skedaddled across the gravel as if he were being chased by those hounds of his. He made it back to his yard in less time than it would've taken to yell "scaredy cat." Then he awkwardly climbed one of the cedar trees outside the fence, jumped from there into his yard and disappeared from sight.

Huh. Why was he suddenly so terrified? Why was he so afraid to be alone with me—caught, caged, incapable-of-harming-a-hair-on-his-head me? I sat and curled my smelly, bedraggled tail around me, puzzling over his strange behavior. I wanted to discuss this entire situation with Alice in a more reasonable manner. Perhaps she'd come back and keep me company now that Felix, the *real* troublemaker, was out of the way.

But she'd already jumped over Emma's fence and had settled onto the porch. There she sat, licking her paws and smoothing her whiskers, seemingly intent on ignoring me while she waited for Twila to take her home.

I stalked back to the chicken house, still stewing about the injustice of it all. Alice would probably never come back for a visit now. And who was to blame? One lying, thieving, conniving kitten!

Why did Felix have such a vendetta against me anyway? I *had* tried to be neighborly when we first met, after all. And come to think of it, why had Lil overreacted so badly when she'd found me in her living room? Did she really believe that I was threatening Felix's safety? That just didn't make sense either. After all, if *Emma* had found *Felix* in her living room, she would've given him the boot out the front door and that would've been the end of that. It was clear that I was dealing with a deranged feline and a slightly unhinged human.

I turned around in the smelly straw, trying to find a more comfortable position. Humph. If Lil were really that unbalanced, maybe I *should* have clawed the furniture. Maybe then she *would* have packed up her animals and left, Emma or no Emma. But that didn't help me now.

I curled into a tight ball and tucked my head under my tail, determined to shut out the world for the moment. There was a lot I didn't understand, but I knew one thing for certain: Felix might think he had my surrender, but I'd not yet begun to fight.

Chapter Fifteen
Put on Probation

I awoke the next morning with the roosters, so to say. Except that there were no roosters in residence. Only one very stiff cat. Sleeping in old, trampled straw, after all, is not nearly as comfortable as sleeping in my own bed of towels.

I had a good stretch starting at the front toes, working through my ears and up my back, and then along to the very tip of my tail. After that, I had an extra long grooming session. It took awhile to get rid of all that chicken fluff since it kind of choked me up. Then all I had left to do was wait for Emma.

And wait. And wait.

When she finally came out of the house, she was carrying the milking pail and had her eyes firmly fixed on the barn. I gave a few pitiful meows, and she finally looked my way.

She frowned but changed direction. "George," she said, taking hold of the latch to the chicken pen. "You'd better behave yourself and stay far, far away from that other cat. If you cause another ruckus, you'll be shipped back to town in nothing flat."

She opened the gate, and I slipped out as fast as I could, just in case she changed her mind. But then I hesitated. Which way should I go? I obviously couldn't mount a frontal assault on that sneaky feline and his two hounds or Emma would send me packing. And morning was not the best time for missions involving stealth.

I glanced toward the corrals. Pauline had already taken the sheep to pasture for the day. She'd probably wondered why I hadn't shown up for report last evening. I frowned, hoping she hadn't heard rumors of my exploits. Then I looked back over my shoulder at Emma's garage. Maybe I should trot over there, have some breakfast, and do some more spying on Felix from my favorite tree. That seemed like the best plan.

Until I saw Jason letting the dogs out of his yard.

Immediately, I changed my mind. It was a much shorter distance to the barn. I galloped after Emma and squeezed into the dim interior just as she was sliding the door closed.

"What's your hurry, George?" Emma asked then stopped and shook her finger at me. "You keep away from Eloise's milk, you hear?"

Humph. I lifted my tail and looked away with as much dignity as I could muster. I hadn't even been *thinking* about Aunt Eloise's milk. But now that she mentioned it, I was feeling a little hungry.

I decided to stop by the feed room to see if I could catch a mouse unaware. And when I peeked in the room, one was sitting in the corner, busily nibbling a kernel of corn and completely unaware of my presence. Perfect. With two bounds, I trapped it against the wall. It was a nice fat one, well plumped from eating all that corn. I gathered myself for a final spring—

—and heard the barn door slide open again. It startled me enough that I turned my head just a tiny bit toward the noise. The mouse noticed the movement, instantly dropped his meal, and slipped like a shadow into a crack between the floorboards.

So much for a snack before breakfast. I flattened my ears and stalked to the feed room door. Who was the wise guy making all the noise?

Peering out of the room, I saw Jason enter the barn—followed by the pair of dogs. Quickly, I pulled my head back out of sight. I'd assumed that the barn would be off limits to those nitwits, just like the old house was now off limits to me. But evidently they, unlike me, could go anywhere they pleased.

I sat perfectly still, listening to Jason's footsteps become fainter as they walked away from me and toward the stanchions, where Emma was milking the cow. I could barely hear him as he asked Emma a question. Something about paint thinner.

Emma answered, but she must've had her face pointed toward the cow, and I couldn't hear what she said at all.

Jason's footsteps became louder again. "…just look around myself. Thanks for your help." As his words became clearer, I also began to notice the light thud of paws. Eight of them, to be exact. And definitely headed in this direction.

I looked around the room. Not many bags of feed to hide behind, no windows, no holes. Even the set of shelves in the corner didn't have enough stuff to provide cover. I grimaced. The minute those dogs entered the room, they would see me, clear as day, and I didn't trust that human to call them off until it was too late. For all I knew, Jason was a Felix sympathizer, too.

Well, there was only one alternative. The rafters. I quickly launched myself to the top of the shelves and from there hooked my claws into an angled board that slanted from stud to stud against the wall. I climbed this brace until I reached a ledge where a window used to be, although it had been boarded over long ago. The ledge was high enough that I could see a rafter not far above me.

By now, Jason's footsteps were almost at the door. I had no choice. I took a deep breath and *sprang*. I barely caught the edge of the rafter with my toenails and hung on for dear life, my back legs clawing and kicking the air underneath. Finally one of them swung close enough to the board to gain hold, and I scrambled to the top.

Just in time.

Jason entered the room with those two bruisers following him. I held my breath and froze into a crouch above him. As I suspected, he didn't have an inkling that I was there. Once humans have their minds set on something, they rarely notice anything but what they're searching for.

He glanced around the room at eye level only, walked to the set of shelves, scooted some cans around, and finally picked one up. He seemed to take a long time reading the label. 'Course, I'm not surprised. Some of those cans have been there since before I was born. The labels are starting to disintegrate.

I was about ready to turn blue from lack of oxygen when he finally moved. "Come on, boys," he said, his eyes still fixed on the can he was holding, and he walked out of the room. I could hear his footsteps growing fainter as he headed toward the barn door.

I let out my breath. Safe!

No, not quite.

The dogs didn't seem so eager to follow. They'd been sniffing the floor in a random, disinterested way, but suddenly Festus' nose appeared to get stuck in one spot, as though he'd found a patch of glue. He whined, and immediately his long-legged companion bounded over to check it out, too.

I had a bad feeling about this.

Both of them began circling, noses to the ground, until Festus went rigid. He'd found the place where I'd been sitting only moments before. He made a beeline for the shelves and then stopped so suddenly that Brutus plowed right over the top of him.

Idiots.

After they'd untangled themselves, they started to sniff in circles. Wrinkling his already well-wrinkled forehead, Festus sat down. "He's here, Brute, I'm sure of it. The scent is only minutes old."

Now I was the one who went rigid. I knew that dogs could follow a trail, of course, but I had no idea they could tell the scent was fresh. It was becoming clear that I lacked some important information about dogs. But maybe, just maybe, the dimwits wouldn't think to look up.

No such luck. After scanning the walls, they both put their snouts in the air, and...well, I was pretty obvious. The rafter didn't have any hidey-holes, after all.

I should've just sat still and stayed calm. There was no way they could reach me from way down there since dogs are equipped with inferior claws that can't be used to climb. Poor beasts. However, being confronted with sharp teeth and slavering jaws, I found it difficult to remain detached from the situation. I did what any cat is programmed to do: I poofed my fur, showed my fangs, and hissed.

Of course that made them do what dogs are programmed to do: bark louder, jump higher, run around in circles, attempt to climb the walls, etc. etc. I'm sure, judging from their performance, that they imagined they could grow wings and fly up to get me if they only tried hard enough. Dogs are obviously programmed to be idiots. But I figured their carryings-on would at least bring one of the humans to my rescue.

Instead, it brought Aunt Eloise.

Chapter Sixteen
Closing the Jaws of Death

Aunt Eloise shambled through the feed room door, licking the morning milk off her whiskers. Then she plumped down in the middle of the floor and began to scrub her face with a paw, completely ignoring the ruckus.

I panicked, unsure of what to do. If I yelled for her to take cover, the dogs would turn and notice her. So far they'd been concentrating on me and were completely unaware of her presence. I stood on my tippy-toes and hissed some more, hoping to keep the yappers' attention on me until either Emma or Jason was attracted to the commotion.

The strategy seemed to work. The dogs began a round of barking and clawing and jumping even more impressive than the last. Unfortunately, it also drew the notice of Aunt Eloise. Her eyes followed the slant of the dogs' noses straight up to me. "Georgie!" she shrilled. "What in tarnation are you doing up there?"

The barking stopped. Brutus and Festus both turned their heads in her direction and went rigid again.

"Aunt Eloise," I yelled. "Run!"

I knew she didn't have much of a chance. She was so old and tottery that the dogs could probably run circles around her. I began to scrabble across the rafter looking for a good spot to claw my way to the ground. "Hey, bozos," I called. "Up here. Remember me?"

But they didn't turn. Instead, they began to growl and edge toward my aunt. I guess to them, a bony cat under paw was worth a bigger one in the bush, or in the rafters as the case may be.

Aunt Eloise had turned her attention from me to the dogs. She made no attempt to run, though—just sat and looked at them. Her eyesight must've been getting as dim as her thinking ability. Maybe she figured they were extra loud sheep or something.

"Aunt Eloise, run! Get out of here before they have you for breakfast!" I yelled. By now, I'd clawed halfway down the wall.

She shook her head. "No need to run." Her eyes broke away from the dogs and planted themselves on me. "You've let this situation get out of control, young man. I told you before to be neighborly, and now you've got these poor critters so worked up, they don't know up from down."

"Aunt Eloise, they don't want conversation. They want breakfast!"

"Well, then. Let's extend an invitation."

Brutus and Festus, meanwhile, had been edging closer and closer to Aunt Eloise, their growls growing louder and more vicious. They hadn't pounced yet, perhaps because their quarry wasn't on the run, but they were within snapping range. Before I could leap to the floor, Brutus went for the kill, chomping at Aunt Eloise with lightning speed, his teeth glinting in the beam of dusty sunlight pouring through the door.

With even more speed, Aunt Eloise's paw flashed forward. Suddenly Brutus' entire body went still.

I'd been in the process of shutting my eyes, afraid to watch as Aunt Eloise became dog chow. Now my eyes went wide, and even wider. Aunt Eloise had hooked her claws on one side of Brutus' snout. As I watched, her other paw flashed forward and hooked the other side.

Brutus went slack and droopy. Festus froze in mid bark.

Aunt Eloise certainly had their attention. She stared into Brutus' eyes as if daring him to move.

He didn't. Instead, he gave a short whine.

"Good." Aunt Eloise twitched her whiskers and dropped her paws. "I'm glad we've come to an understanding. Now boys, would you care to join me at the milking stanchion? If Emma's still there, I'm sure she could be persuaded to give you a taste."

She glanced over at me. "You come, too, George. A little breakfast conversation would do you good."

I took that to be an order.

It was a strange procession that wound through the barn—first Aunt Eloise, wobbling unsteadily, then Brutus and Festus respectfully giving her plenty of space, and then me with narrowed eyes and poofed tail. I couldn't help being suspicious.

But Aunt Eloise seemed to have things completely under control. When we reached the stanchion, she preened and rubbed against Emma's legs until Emma did something entirely un-Emma-like—she rummaged up a couple more bowls and gave us *all* some milk. I couldn't help but notice that this leg rubbing was the same way that Alice had gotten Twila to give her a ride to the farm. Interesting. Perhaps I should study the technique.

Emma watched us for a few moments, her eyebrows lifted as though she couldn't believe what she was seeing. I knew how she felt—I couldn't believe it either. Those hounds were lapping up the milk, polite as could be, giving no sign of having ever desired anything remotely like cat burger.

Then Emma shrugged, picked up her bucket, and left. I wanted to jump in front of her and yowl and make her understand that she needed to take those dogs with her. However, Aunt Eloise had her eye on me, and that eye was saying I'd better sit still.

So I did.

After the milk was finished, Aunt Eloise insisted that the yappers stay and talk a bit. Bleh. Like I was interested in their previous life as city dogs. Small apartment, cement instead of grass, leashes at all times—even in the park. It sounded like torture to me.

"And Felix," Festus rumbled. "Lil wouldn't let him out of the apartment at all. The rest of us would take our walk to the park, and he'd sit in the window watching us go."

Aunt Eloise pricked her ears forward. "Felix? And who might that young man be? A poodle, a Chihuahua?"

"Nope, ma'am," Brutus ducked his head politely. "Felix is a cat. He sure enjoys being out in the sun now that we've moved."

"Ah." Aunt Eloise gave me the eye again. "And why haven't I had the privilege of meeting this Felix?"

Festus cleared his throat. "Well, he's a little nervous about open territory. Doesn't like to leave the porch." Both of the dogs turned their heads and stared at me. Aunt Eloise followed their gaze.

I suddenly became very interested in the barn swallow nest in the rafters above us. I would've coughed up a hairball on those bow-wows' feet if I could've figured out how to do so without arousing Aunt Eloise's ire. Now Aunt Eloise would be on my back about making Felix feel more "at home" when she didn't have all the facts straight.

Fact number one: I'd tried to be neighborly right from the start, but Felix had laughed in my face and then turned the dogs loose.

Fact number two: He'd squashed Emma's coleus, knowing full well that I would take the blame.

Fact number three: He'd laughed in my face—again—when Emma locked me up for taking a snooze in Lil's living room.

I wonder if Aunt Eloise would've been so "neighborly" had she been in my shoes—uh, paws. This was so obviously part of Felix's plot, trying to turn my allies against me. And in the case of Aunt Eloise, it seemed to be working.

"Hmm," she said, her voice prickly as sand burrs. "We'll have to see if we can remedy that."

"Sure thing," I muttered. "Now I have to get back to patrol, if you don't mind, since I've been *detained* for the last couple of days." I aimed a prickly look of my own in the direction of those hounds, tipped my tail in the air and made tracks before Aunt Eloise could ask any more embarrassing questions.

Chapter Seventeen
A Plot Is Uncovered
and a Plan Is Hatched

Leaving the barn, I stalked over to the grain bins to prowl. I *wanted* to be chasing Felix right now—down the lane and out of my life—but instead I settled for shredding an old work glove of Ted's that he'd left lying by the bins. Even after that, I was still seeing red. Aunt Eloise had been duped by those dogs, pure and simple. Now I wouldn't be able to set foot in the barn without her lecturing me about being "nicer" to the neighbors. This was just what Felix and his cohorts wanted: divide and conquer.

Emma came out of her house and headed toward the garden, and I decided to follow her. I hoped catching a few grasshoppers might help my disposition and my empty stomach. But I was so out of temper that the very first time Emma dumped me over the side of the fence, I didn't try to figure out what she wanted. I just left. I didn't even look back to see if she was sorry.

On the way back from the garden, I scrambled up the tree that overlooked my beloved porch and stared daggers at the conniving cat who was sleeping there in my spot. It didn't make sense. Felix obviously had my spot, and there seemed to be no way to boot him out of it. So why was he still coming after me? Why was he turning Emma and Alice and Aunt Eloise against me? Why was he trying so hard to get me out of the way?

And then, all of a sudden, it hit me—like Lil blasting me with water from the hose. It hit me what Emma had said just this morning. She'd said that if I didn't behave, she'd ship me back to town and let Felix take up mouse patrol duties.

That had to be it! Felix wanted to be boss of more than just the porch—he wanted to take over the farm. He wasn't happy with *one* of my spots—he wanted them all.

That thief, that interloper, that conniving beast! The hair on my shoulder began to poof, and I had to lick it back into submission.

The problem was, Felix had no idea what being

"boss" really meant. He didn't know a thing about mouse patrols and rat raids. With him in charge, the rodent population would be out of control within days. The feed shed would be overrun, the animals would starve, and Emma and Ted would go bankrupt! This was an emergency. The safety of the farm was at stake. I definitely needed to get Felix and his buddies out of here before their takeover was complete.

But what could I do now that Lil, Emma, and Aunt Eloise were watching my every move? To them, Felix was just a "sweet, helpless kitty." They had no idea what a hardened con artist was lurking under that cute, whiskered face.

Just thinking about it boiled my bones. If only I could get him alone. If only I could catch him off guard and … and …

Catch him off guard. Hmmm. Now that was an idea. What would catch him off guard? Not a frontal assault. Not an attack from the rear. Not sending in the troops. (I didn't even *have* any troops, unless you counted Aunt Eloise. And she had just defected to the other side.)

But what if …

… what if I gave Felix exactly what he wanted? I

narrowed my eyes and peered through the screen of leaves at the small feline sleeping soundly on the porch below. It might work. Maybe ... just maybe ... the job would scare him more than I ever could.

When I headed to the corrals that evening for Pauline's report, I had the plan outlined and fixed firmly in my mind. It was simple, really. All I had to do was announce my resignation to Felix, tell him he was next in line for the job, and send him out to the pasture with Pauline for his first assignment. I'd get Pauline to make herself scarce for a few minutes and have Felix deal with the sheep on his own. With him being a city cat, I was sure there was enough harmless stuff out there to scare him silly. Rabbits, garter snakes ... good grief, he might even be terrified of the sheep if they wandered too close.

Worst case scenario: By the time Pauline got back, he'd be ready to hand the job (and the sunny spot) back over to me, quit with the "harmless kitty" act, and call off the canines. Best case scenario: If I could get Lil to notice that Felix had been wandering in the pasture, she'd be so afraid for his safety that she'd lock him in the house for the rest of his life. I could always hope.

Pauline was waiting at the gate when I arrived.

"Anything to report?" I asked, although I wasn't expecting anything out of the ordinary. To tell you the truth, I was ready to skip over this part of the proceedings and launch right into my plan.

Pauline pursed her lips. "I saw Old Mangy, or at least a scraggly coyote that looks an awful lot like him."

"What?!" My ears shot forward as all other thoughts vanished. "In our pasture?"

Pauline grimaced. "No, in Harold's pasture across from ours. He was pretty far back. Probably thought he was hidden in the grass." Pauline allowed herself a tight smile. "He hadn't counted on my sharp eyesight, though."

"He's come out of hiding, then."

"I'd say so."

"Must be getting hungry."

"Must be."

Hmm. I twitched my tail and looked toward the old house. How would Old Mangy's appearance affect my plan? It would be a serious situation if he caught that little cat out in the pasture, alone and unprotected. But a coyote would be *way* more scary than a garter snake if I could figure out a way to control the situation.

I stroked my whiskers with a paw. "Pauline, I have

a plan. We can dispatch two birds, that is, two problems, with one stone."

Pauline drew her ears forward. "*Two* problems? Old Mangy is the only problem I'm aware of."

I felt my fur began to poof just thinking about the Felix problem. "Problem number one is Old Mangy, of course," I said. "Problem number two is a certain pipsqueak cat named Felix. Now—"

"A pipsqueak *cat?*" Pauline butted in. "How much of a problem can a *cat* be?"

I flattened my ears, not wanting to go into any embarrassing details. "If only you knew. Now tomorrow, I'm going to pretend to hand all of my duties over to Felix and tell him his first assignment is to go on patrol out in the pasture with you—"

Pauline reared her head. "You want me to take him on patrol?" she spluttered. "I wouldn't even take *you* on patrol with a known killer on the loose. It'd be inviting disaster. It's insanity!"

"Just let me finish, okay?" I said, pulling my whiskers downward.

Pauline put her lips together in a straight line, and even though she was going cross-eyed with the effort, she didn't open them.

"This will work," I insisted. "All you have to do is turn your back for a second, and if Old Mangy's around, it'll make him think you're not looking. He'll sneak over, scare Felix half to death, and be taken by surprise when you come running to the rescue. When the dust has cleared, Felix'll be desperate to return command of the farm to me."

Pauline tilted her nose downward. "Return command? You're absolutely right. By the time Old Mangy gets done with him, he'll be returning command for sure—from the depths of Old Mangy's stomach!"

I smiled lazily. "That, my dear friend, is impossible. There's not a coyote around who can outsmart you. You said yourself that you'd spotted the beast before he was even in our pasture."

Pauline snorted and glared down at me. "And how is putting this feline directly in the path of danger going to help our situation with Old Mangy?"

I grinned. "Think of it as waiting in ambush while Felix acts as the bait. By the time Old Mangy realizes you're aware of him, you'll be close enough to catch him before he reaches the fence." I tilted my head and grinned at her. "If you're fast enough."

"If I'm fast enough?" Pauline jerked her head

straight in the air. "I'm faster than any flea-bitten coyote."

"Well, then. It's all set." I stood and stretched. "I'll have Felix out to the pasture by midmorning tomorrow. If you see Old Mangy, try to lure him to the middle of the pasture, away from all the fences so you'll have plenty of room to catch him. Got it?"

Pauline stared at me for a long moment. "I suppose," she said, her nose still wrinkled. "But—"

"Great," I said. "I'll come out to the pasture, hopefully with a human in tow, to fetch Felix back after the big scare. Just try to keep an eye on him until I get there." I turned and began to pad toward the garage.

Pauline called after me. "It'll only take one snap of the jaws, and he's done for."

"He'll be fine," I said over my shoulder. "You've never lost a sheep. How could you lose a cat?"

I heard her snort again but I didn't stop. She was a professional; I could count on her. And I needed my sleep. It was going to take every bit of my persuasive ability to convince Felix to go on patrol in the pasture tomorrow.

My tail twitched. It was going to be an unforgettable experience for that wimpy feline.

Chapter Eighteen
A Plan and a Pancake

I tried to look casual as I wandered by the old house the next morning. Pausing in a conspicuous spot, I pretended to lick a sticker off my paw.

The dogs saw me instantly and raised a commotion, barking and slavering their way to the fence just as I'd hoped. Felix had been dozing in my spot on the porch, but his eyes snapped open when the ruckus began. He slowly stretched full length then sat and swiped at his fur with his tongue. When the dogs noticed him sitting, they stopped barking and trotted up the steps to take their positions on either side of him.

"So you were finally let out of the pen, huh?" Felix said, raising a paw and examining it as though some speck of dirt might've escaped him. "Too bad your little adventure scared your girlfriend away." He looked at me and crinkled his nose.

I felt myself begin to puff up, and it was all I could do to keep my hair flat and voice steady. It was probably better not to bring up the obvious—that Alice had stalked off because she was disgusted with Felix for picking a fight with me. The entire situation wouldn't have happened if Felix hadn't nosed his way into the middle of it. The little upstart needed to scram. And soon.

"Oh, that," I said with all the calm I could muster. "It was a big misunderstanding. I'm on my way to patch things up with Alice right now."

Felix's whiskers twitched. "Old man, you need glasses. She's nowhere in the area."

"Nope," I agreed. "I'm on my way to town. Just thought I'd stop and say good-bye."

"Good-bye?" Felix pitched his ears so far forward that the tips were practically touching.

"Yeah, this is it, kid. The moment you've been waiting for. I'm tired of hubbub and false accusations and human misunderstanding. I've turned in my resignation and am heading back to town. Twila will take me in, I'm sure. And like I said, I can smooth out the situation with Alice."

"You're ... you're resigning?"

"That's right. And I'm turning the whole mess over to you. Effective immediately. There's no other cat on the place who's physically able to handle the job. My aunt"— I jerked my head toward the barn —"is in no condition to be on the prowl, as your two compatriots can tell you." I shrugged. "Congratulations, kid. It's the promotion you've been waiting for."

Felix's eyes went huge. "I've been waiting for this?"

I shook my head. "Listen, you've been after me since the moment you arrived, hoping to get your claws into my job. Well, now it's yours."

"B-b-b-but ..."

"No need to act ignorant. I've known almost from Day One what you were up to. And now you have it. By the way, Pauline is waiting for you out in the pasture. She wants to brief you on your duties."

"Pauline? B-b-b-but ..."

"No buts, kid. You're in charge. Pauline's your second-in-command. A llama. Big, shaggy, long neck ... you can't miss her. She's on duty in the pasture and she's waiting. It's time for you to shoulder your responsibilities."

I would've been pleased at the look of horror on the

other cat's face if I hadn't known it was an act. Judging by Felix's rigid tail and whiskers, I figured he'd been practicing hard for this moment. Part of the "poor little kitty" routine.

I stood and took my time stretching the kinks out of my hind legs. "I have a long walk ahead of me, so I'd better get started. By the way—" I turned and nodded toward the dogs— "don't think about bringing the canines along to the pasture. They'll terrorize the sheep, and you don't want Pauline mad at you from the get-go." I lifted my whiskers in what I hoped passed for a smile. "Good luck."

Then I wandered down the lane without looking back. When I'd gone out of sight of the house, I stopped and glanced in all directions to make sure no one was around before clambering to the top of a bushy tree. I could see the entire farmyard from here, but Felix and his pals wouldn't be able to see me.

Felix was still sitting on the porch exactly where I'd left him. He sat and sat and sat so long that I was getting worried that he might not play along. Maybe he was more savvy about the danger in the pasture than I thought.

"Come on, kid," I muttered. "You wanted the job. Get going!"

The sun was *much* higher in the sky (and I was about ready to fall asleep from lack of action) when he finally moved from the porch to the yard. The dogs trotted after him, but he must've said something because the pair of canines stopped short of the fence. They watched their little friend scramble awkwardly up the chain links and drop down, stiff-legged, on the other side. Brutus put his front legs on the fence and jumped and wiggled and wagged for a bit, but Felix shook his head and began to pick his way very slowly across the gravel toward the barn.

Petrified, I thought. *The kid looks petrified.* And I felt a twinge of guilt. But then I remembered the little beast laughing at me through the chicken wire of the pen, and I quickly regained my focus.

It was all an act. The kid was a superb actor. He was probably just being dramatic for the sake of the dogs. If he made this task look life-threatening, they would be even more slavishly loyal when he returned home, cool and composed, as the conquering hero. Little did he know that he wouldn't return so cool and composed.

I narrowed my eyes and pulled further under cover of the leaves.

Felix stopped short of the barn and looked back over his shoulder like he was seriously considering turning around. But at last he gave himself a shake and scooted into the tall grass between the shop and the barn, disappearing from view.

I let out my breath, not even realizing that I'd been holding it. Perfect. He was heading to the pasture just as planned. Or at least I hoped he was heading to the pasture. It wasn't the way I would've gone, but come to think of it, I hadn't exactly given him directions. Oh, well. Once he got beyond the barn, there wasn't anywhere else he could go. Pauline would find him because she was aware of everything that happened in that pasture. Felix was in capable hands.

Now for the hardest part of my scheme. I needed to alert Lil that her precious "kitty" was in harm's way. I eyed the yard where the dogs were still sitting, their snouts pushed up against the chain links. Maybe I could use them as an alarm.

I climbed quietly down from the tree. Then, taking a deep breath, I let out an ear-splitting yowl and dashed into the farmyard as though Old Mangy himself were after me. The dogs saw me and instantly began to bark and paw at the fence. I poofed my tail and hissed. As

I'd hoped, this added to their excitability. They woofed and bayed and jumped against the fence even harder, crashing into it just like insects ramming a lightbulb at night.

Idiots.

The screen door banged open, and Lil poked her head out. "Hush up, you idiots."

Ha! Even Lil knew that her dogs were idiots! But the dogs ignored her, carrying on with the din.

Lil stepped onto the porch. "I can't hear myself think. What's going on out there?" And then she saw me. "Why you dirty little …"

I poofed my fur even more. Who did she think she was, calling me dirty? The mention of dirt, however, seemed to give the canines an idea. Brutus' barks switched to maniacal growls, and he began digging furiously under the fence. Festus joined him. Chunks of grass and soil were flying everywhere.

"Stop that!" Lil shouted. She charged down the walk with amazing speed, grabbed Brutus' collar and hauled him backward. "Stop that!" she shouted again, giving him a clunk on the nose.

Brutus whined and slunk far enough away to be out of her reach then crouched and rumbled low in his throat. Festus also attempted a crouch, but tripped over an ear.

Lil glared at them and then at me. "Get out of here, you nasty cat. Get. Get!" She stooped and picked up a handful of the newly disturbed dirt.

This plan was working perfectly. Now I just needed to get her to open the gate and follow me. I dodged the dirt and launched myself toward a tree next to the gate. Scrabbling onto one of the bottom branches, I stood on my tippy-toes and let out an ear-splitting hiss. Like clockwork, the dogs began another round of barking and bouncing and tearing at the grass. As I've said, dogs are programmed to be idiots.

Idiots or not, their ruckus produced the desired effects. Lil threw the next handful of dirt at the yappers instead of me and flung open the gate. The dogs bulldozed around her, almost knocking her to the ground.

I leaped from the tree and began to dash across the farm yard, keeping my eyes on the dogs to make sure they were still following me. Suddenly I heard a loud screech that sounded exactly like someone stomping on the brakes of a vehicle. I whipped my head around and saw a car tire—a very large car tire that was rapidly becoming even larger—spewing gravel from either side as it came straight toward me. I was only a whisker away from being turned into a kitty pancake!

Chapter Nineteen
Second Thoughts

Instantly I leaned back on my haunches and extended my claws, hoping for some braking action of my own. My claws didn't make much headway in the soft gravel though, so instead of stopping, I lost my balance and tumbled directly under the vehicle just as it pulled to a full stop.

I yowled and leaped to my feet, hitting my head on the undercarriage and knocking myself over again.

Lil yelled.

The dogs howled.

Then the driver's door opened and a pair of feet jumped out. "Good heavens!" a voice called. "Is everyone okay?"

I was feeling slightly bleary from the bonk to my head so I couldn't be positive, but the voice sure sounded like Twila's.

"That nasty … that horrible cat …" Lil's voice carried over the cacophony. "He almost killed my dogs." Footsteps stumbled toward the car, and Lil's face peeked underneath. "He's still alive," she said, sounding a little disappointed.

"Thank goodness!" the voice exclaimed. Yep, now I was sure it was Twila's voice. "How would I ever explain it to Emma if I ran over her best cat?"

Then something swiped at my shoulder, and I jerked.

"George!" My eyes focused on Alice, who was prodding me with a paw. "George, are you okay? Talk to me, George!"

I gingerly pulled myself upright. "I seem to be in one piece."

Alice plunked down next to me. "You almost gave me heart failure!" she said.

"That makes two of us." I looked down and saw that my fur had exploded into the grand-daddy of all poofs.

"Poor George," Alice said, and began licking me. "You look a little worked up."

"No wonder," I retorted. "I just missed being flattened into a pancake."

"I noticed," she said, and rubbed against me with her

shoulder, which I'm sure was meant to calm me down but instead made me feel all wobbly inside. Then she gave my ears one more lick, not helping my wobbles at all, and said "Let's get out from under here, okay?"

"Good idea," I said, and tottered to my feet.

I heard some hysterics still going on above me. Lil was clinging to the hood of the car, accusing me of all kinds of violent crimes while Twila patted her shoulder. But they didn't try to stop me from leaving, thank heavens. Alice followed me across the gravel to the strip of grass in front of Emma's fence. We both sat, and I leaned against the railings. My legs had gone all twitchy and trembly.

"Didn't you hear us coming?" Alice asked.

I shook my head. "No. I was right in the middle of a dog chase. All I heard was a bunch of barking."

Alice looked at me sympathetically. "You still haven't worked things out with Felix, have you?"

"Ha!" The word burst out before I could stop it. "I was right in the middle of trying to work something out when I was almost flattened." I began licking my fur and Alice joined me. The rhythm of our tongues gradually steadied me. I could feel my coat shrinking to normal size.

Alice must've felt me relax. She stopped licking and quietly watched me smooth a particularly stubborn patch of fur on my paw. "I think you and Felix should have a good talk," she said suddenly.

"What?" I stopped, my paw still in midair.

"You should talk, you know."

"I've tried," I growled. "And he just sends the dogs after me."

"And he told me that when he's tried talking with you, all you can do is give orders."

"What?" I said again. The hair on my paw poofed back on end. I glared at it, then put the offending foot on the ground and turned my narrowed eyes on Alice. "That's the biggest lie I've ever heard. He's trying to bamboozle you the same as he's done with Emma and Lil. I'm telling you …"

"George, just listen for once, okay? Just listen. I know you're used to being in charge. I know you're used to giving orders. But Felix isn't used to taking orders. He's barely more than a kitten, right?"

She stared at me until I reluctantly nodded. Then she tilted her head. "Don't you remember what it's like to be young?"

"Of course I remember!" I burst out. "That's when

Emma brought me here and Aunt Eloise began my training. If I'd been as snooty as Felix, Aunt Eloise would've tossed me out on my ear. She'd never have given me this responsibility!"

"You're lucky," Alice said.

"Luck has nothing to do with it," I spat. "I worked hard. I did what I was told. I learned."

Alice shook her head. "That's not what I meant. You were lucky because you had someone to teach you."

I glared at her. "I was willing to be taught. Felix has no desire to learn anything."

"I disagree." Alice wrapped her tail primly around herself. "He wants to learn. He *really* wants to learn. But he doesn't know how."

I frowned.

"Just think about it, George. The poor kid was taken away from his mom when he was just tiny. He was locked inside an apartment with only a human and two dogs for company. He'd never even been *outside* 'til he moved here."

She paused. I looked away. This was all a bunch of nonsense. The kid was such a good actor, he'd even fooled Alice into feeling sorry for him.

Alice waited for a moment before continuing. "He told me that the first time he'd stepped foot out the door, he was so overwhelmed by all the new sounds and smells and feels that he couldn't stand it. He had to go right back in the house. It took him several tries just to get used to sitting on the porch."

She nudged me with her head. "And when he walked out to the chicken pen to visit you? That was the first time he'd ever stepped onto gravel."

I flicked my tail. This was all nonsense. The kid was a conniving …

And then a picture popped into my mind. A memory of the first time I'd been inside the barn with Aunt Eloise. I remembered how huge the building had seemed—like a dark, damp, frightening cave. I could still feel the way the cool air had almost slapped me on the face, heavy with unfamiliar scents of dusty straw, fresh milk, and rodent remains. The doves cooing in the rafters had thrown me into a panic.

I closed my eyes. What if Alice was right? What if Felix wasn't *acting* scared? What if he really *was* scared?

No. He couldn't really be scared. He'd never have agreed to go out to the pasture by himself.

But it had taken him a long time to get over the

fence—to walk across the farm yard.

My eyes flew open. He hadn't *acted* petrified. He'd *been* petrified. And even so, he'd somehow found the courage to walk out to the pasture alone. The kid had guts. I'd give him that.

And I'd sent him to the pasture to get the scare of his life. When he came home, he'd never want to go outside again. Lil would never let him go outside again. He'd be in a—a prison—for the rest of his life because of *me*.

I rubbed at my face with a paw. When I put the paw down, Alice was still watching me. I rose to my feet and stretched, front to back. "Well," I said. "I think it's time for a long talk with Felix. Would you like to come along?"

Chapter Twenty
Too Late for Apologies

"Why are you going that way?" Alice asked as I began trotting toward the barn.

I looked over my shoulder at her. "What?"

She pointed her nose toward the old house. "Felix's place is over there, right?"

I stopped short, realizing that Alice didn't know what I'd sent Felix off to do. "Uh," I said. "He's not at the house. He went out to explore the pasture with Pauline this morning."

"The pasture?" Alice's eyes rounded. "I had to do a lot of talking just to get him over to the chicken pen a couple of days ago. What gave him the spunk to go out to the *pasture*?"

"Uh," I said again. My mind was spewing out possible things I could say, the truth being first choice, of course. But somehow my tongue wasn't cooperating. And I needed to find Felix fast, before he reached maximum overload, right? I'd have to talk with Alice about this later.

"Not sure," I told her, which wasn't *quite* a lie. After all, I had no idea where the kid had come up with the gumption to go out there by himself. "But if he's as scared as you say, we'd better go get him before he has a panic attack and decides he doesn't want to set foot out of his yard again." Which was what I'd originally wanted, but no way was I going to tell Alice *that*. At least, not now.

We got all the way to the barn before I realized something was wrong. It was barely lunch time, but the sheep were already crowding into the corral from the pasture. Pauline never brought them in this early.

I narrowed my eyes and watched them as they milled around, bleating.

"Great," I said.

"What's the matter?" asked Alice.

"I told Pauline that I'd come out to the pasture to fetch Felix, and since I didn't arrive, Pauline must have decided to bring him back herself."

"Is that a bad thing?"

"Well …" I scratched an ear. "I suppose not, except it probably means that Felix has reached overload already. If he was able to keep himself under control, there'd be no reason to bring him back."

"So we might be too late?"

I looked at Alice. Her whiskers were drooping.

I tried to keep my whiskers from doing the same. "No way to tell for sure until we have Pauline's report. Come on," I said. "Let's meet them."

I hopped easily over the bottom bar of the corral gate, glanced back to make sure Alice was following, then trotted along the edge of the pen by the barn. The sheep knew me, and on a normal day, they wouldn't have done more than turn their heads in my direction. But today they bolted away, raising clouds of dust as they circled and huddled together.

What was wrong with them?

My fur—and my nerves—were starting to feel the same as that time I'd been caught outside in the middle of a lightning storm. Snappish and crackly. Heated up like I was about to get struck by something bad. Really bad.

I lengthened my stride so that my trot was now a full fledged gallop.

As I reached the open pasture gate, the last of the sheep were crowding their way into the corral. I dodged their hooves and clawed my way to the top of a fence post where I might get a good view of Pauline.

I scanned the area. "Uh …"

"What's wrong?" asked Alice from below me.

"I don't see Pauline. Or Felix, either." I glanced around the corral. Surely they hadn't come through the gate without me noticing.

Alice sat. "It's a big pasture, right?"

"Yeah. But Pauline always stays right with the sheep. She doesn't let them wander out of her sight."

"So …?"

"So, something's wrong." I jumped back to the ground. "We need more information."

I looked around. One of the sheep standing nearby seemed slightly calmer than her pals.

"Hey," I called to her. "Can I ask you a question?"

The sheep lowered her head and bellowed, "Baaaaa." Not an encouraging sign.

I slowly sat, attempting to look nonthreatening, but kept my muscles tensed and ready to spring out of the way if she decided to charge at me. "It's okay. Really. I'm a friend," I said in as soothing a voice as I could muster. "I just need to know where Pauline has gone."

"Pauline," she blatted. "Pauline. She told us to get back to the barn. She stayed to find the little one. She had to find the little one before the coyote did."

As she said "coyote," she rolled her eyes, and when she focused on me again, she was looking a little wild around the edges, as if she thought *I* might be the coyote.

"Alice, let's get out of here," I said quickly, and pushed her under the bottom board of the fence. When I glanced back, the sheep had already disappeared within the flock.

"Did she say *coyote?*" Now Alice's fur was beginning to poof.

"Yes." Again, I glanced across the pasture. And my heart did a jump. I could see Pauline now, coming over a little rise, still a good distance away. "Stay here," I said, and quickly raced toward the llama. As I got closer, I could see she was walking behind a lamb, encouraging it to keep going as it wobbled and stumbled along.

"Pauline," I shouted. "Pauline!"

She swiveled her neck and looked down her nose to find me. "George, thank heavens you're here. You have to call off your plan immediately. You absolutely *can't* send that other cat—"

"What?" I cut in. "Felix wasn't out there with you?"

Pauline stopped. The lamb plopped to the ground in front of her. "I haven't seen hide nor hair of any cat except you today. And her." She pointed her nose, and I looked around. Alice was picking her way through the wiry grass to join us.

"But you *had* to have seen him," I said, my voice sounding tight as if I were trying to push it through a very small space. "He left for the pasture almost an hour ago."

Pauline studied me. "An hour ago?"

"Yes! I saw him myself. He walked between the barn and the machine shed and …"

"And …" Pauline prompted.

"And then I lost sight of him. But there's nothing back there except the pasture. How could he just disappear?"

"George," Pauline said. "If he's out there—"She nodded her head back the way she'd come. "—he's in big trouble. Old Mangy showed up not long ago. Scattered the sheep and scared them witless. Created enough commotion that I didn't notice he'd cut a lamb out of the flock until it was almost too late. I sent the rest of the flock back and drove Old Mangy through the fence to get him away from the lamb."

She looked at me.

"So Old Mangy's gone for the moment," I said.

"For the moment," she agreed. "But a fence has never meant much to him before."

I frowned. "If Felix is alone out there …"

"I can only confirm that the coyote is on the loose. Felix …?" Pauline shook her head. "Well, I hope he had the sense to head home."

I huffed through my whiskers, thinking quickly, then looked over at Alice. "I need your help," I said. "I need you to go back to Lil's and find out if Felix is there. If he is, just stay and keep him company till I get back. If he isn't …" I paused. "If he isn't back, I need you to get somebody out to the pasture to look for us, ASAP."

"But how—" she started.

I cut her off. "Do whatever you have to do. That move you did, weaving through Twila's legs the other day. Do that, or make sad eyes at her, or *something*. Get the dogs to help if you have to."

She tilted her head. "But why can't you—"

"I'm heading out to the pasture," I said. "With Pauline, if she'll come along. We've got to assume that Felix is still out there and that it's not too late."

"No—" began Alice.

"Hold on," said Pauline.

"We don't have time to argue!" I shouted.

Pauline butted the lamb to its feet. "George, I can't go anywhere with you until I get this lamb back to his mother. He's my responsibility. I'll be glad to accompany you after he's safely returned."

I looked back toward the corrals. Then I looked at the lamb, ready to drop from exhaustion into the grass again.

"It'll take time," I said.

Pauline dipped her head. "It will."

"I can't afford the time. I'll have to go alone."

"But—" Alice said.

"No arguments," I said firmly. "Felix is my responsibility just like the lamb is Pauline's." I started to trot away. "Come find me," I called over my shoulder. "Hopefully I can hold off a coyote long enough for one of you to bring in a rescue party!"

I didn't wait to see what they might do next. I just ran.

Chapter Twenty-One
To the Rescue

"Felix!" I called as I ran. "Felix, we've got to talk!" I paused for a moment and swiveled my super tuned ears.

There was nothing.

I made a mad dash for a distant clump of tall grass and called again. Still nothing. I cautiously peered from the grass and studied the lay of the land. The pasture was a long one. It covered the distance between the barn and the end of the lane, a good mile away. And it wasn't a flat piece of ground. With all the rolls and dips of the hills along the way, there was no way I could see to the farthest end.

I streaked from one clump of grass to another, calling, "Felix! Felix come on out. This is no trick. We have to talk!"

I held my breath and listened to the silence. It was so quiet. Too quiet. "Felix!" I yelled. "Answer me before we both become someone's dinner!"

I plowed through another patch of thick grass and peered out of the other side, listening, straining for any peep that might signal Felix's location.

Then I heard it—a thin mewl like a kitten in distress.

As fast as if Old Mangy himself were chasing me, I dashed in the direction of that cry, tail whipping behind me, ears swiveling to pinpoint the location. "Hold on, Felix," I panted, "I'm coming!" It felt like I was running forever. My trembling legs seemed about ready to collapse.

Then I topped a small hill and saw something gray and fuzzy in the grass at the bottom. It was Felix! He was curled into a ball, hunched as far as he could get from the shaggy, slavering hulk of a coyote that was crouched above him. Old Mangy himself.

"Come on!" the coyote was laughing, clawing at the Felix bundle. "You're not being any fun. Hiss a little. Claw a little. Let's have a tussle!"

He laughed again and picked Felix up by the scruff of the neck with his gleaming teeth, giving him a good shake before thunking the small cat onto the ground.

Felix squealed and tucked himself up tighter.

I shook my head. The kid didn't even have the brains to try to make a break for it. But maybe he'd already tried and found out there's no escape. I glanced around. What was I going to do?

"OK, I guess the game's over. Lunchtime!" howled the hairy bully.

There was no time to make a plan. I did the first thing that popped into my head. Coiling my super charged legs beneath me, I sprang into the air and sailed down the small hill, landing squarely on Old Mangy's furry grey back. Quickly, I dug in my claws.

The coyote immediately whipped around to see who was taking a ride. I held on desperately.

"Run, Felix!" I screamed. "Get out of here while you can!"

The gray ball uncurled, and an eye peeked out at me.

"Go!"

He stretched out and tried to obey, but his back legs weren't working quite right. There was a huge gash on his side, and he could barely drag himself through the grass. No wonder the kid hadn't tried to run.

Now what?

Old Mangy was whirling around, snapping at me and kicking up dry grass and sand in a whirlwind that stung my eyes. If I came loose, Felix and I were both goners. I sank my fangs into his shaggy coat, trying to get a better grip, even though I was barely able to breathe through the hide. But my bite whipped the hairy brute into a bigger frenzy. He began howling and growling and snapping with such ferocity that even though I was doing my best to make like a sand burr, I began slowly and steadily to slide down his flank.

OK, I said to myself as I started to fall. If I'm going to be lunch, I'll at least make it one to remember!

My claws made furrows down Old Mangy's side as I slipped further. At the last moment I let go and landed on the ground, perfectly balanced on all four feet. The great grey beast came at me with jaws snapping, but I dodged out of the way and raked his nose with my claws.

Old Mangy howled again and launched at me so quickly that I couldn't fling myself out of the way. Desperately I twisted, causing his teeth to rake across my side instead of going around my throat. As his tail flashed past, I clamped down on it with my teeth, locking my jaws as tightly as possible around the stinky, scroungy hair. (Bleh. If I got through this alive, I'd need several bowls of water to wash out the taste!)

The coyote leaped into the air, growling and whining, then whipped his tail back and forth so violently that I finally had to let go—that or risk a broken neck. The force of it rolled me the rest of the way down the hill and I landed with a hard thunk against a fence post there.

My brain kicked into overdrive. The fence post meant that we were at the very edge of Emma's pasture. Pauline might not even find us way out here—or at least might not find us in time.

I jumped to my feet, trying to ignore the stinging gash on my side, and braced myself for another charge. But Old Mangey was heading away from me. What was going on? Was he giving up, or was this some kind of trick?

Narrowing my eyes and ready to spring out of the way at even the hint of a tail's twitch, I watched the coyote nosing around in the grass. And then I realized—the brute was following Felix's trail.

Glancing ahead, I could see the little cat straining and pulling his back legs behind him, doing his best to get away. But he wasn't going nearly fast enough, and he wasn't even heading for the cover of trees around the fence line. He was making for open pasture.

"Felix!" I yelled. "Turn around. Get yourself over to a tree!" And I launched myself up the hill, spitting and hissing, poofing myself into one huge orange ball of fangs and claws.

The effect was excellent. Old Mangy took one look at me and backed up a step or two. But it only took a split second for him to remember that he had teeth and claws, too—and his were bigger.

He charged at me and I was forced to veer out of the way. His back flashed by so quickly that I wasn't able to jump on top of him again. Before I could turn for another pass, I felt a set of teeth clamp down on *my* tail. I screeched, and the sound of it was enough to curl my toes—or maybe my toes were already curled because of the pain. My yowling, however, didn't startle the coyote into letting go.

I whirled around and launched myself at his face, spitting and clawing, but with one jerk of my tail, he knocked me off my feet. My head hit the ground with a thump, and I saw stars—and they weren't the ones up in the sky, if you know what I mean.

Old Mangy let go of my tail and pinned me to the ground with a paw. "Bye-bye," he laughed, and he opened his jaws. Time seemed to stretch and slow as his teeth descended. I could smell his putrid breath.

Told you so, Aunt Eloise, I thought. Too much bravery is *not* a good thing. I'd like to see you get out of this situa—

Wait! What would Aunt Eloise do?

Frantically, I jerked one paw loose and whapped it onto the side of Old Mangy's muzzle. He jumped in surprise, which allowed me enough time to loosen my other paw.

Old Mangy growled and began to shake his head, but before he could work himself free, I whapped him on the other side of the muzzle with my other paw. It wasn't exactly pleasant holding onto the smelly beast in such close quarters, but inhaling nasty coyote breath was better than being chomped by nasty coyote teeth.

The varmint had stopped shaking his head. In fact, he'd gone quite rigid.

I looked him straight in the eye just like I'd seen Aunt Eloise do with Brutus. "I think you need a lesson in manners."

Old Mangy started to laugh, but I dug my claws

into his sensitive skin even further. The laugh changed to a whine. "Please," he said. "*Please* let me go."

"Ha!" I said. "The manners are kicking in already. However, I'm guessing you might need some advanced instruction before it's safe to set you free." And I was needing some advanced help. Someone a little bigger than the coyote. Where was Pauline? Or Emma?

We stared at each other.

Old Mangy broke the silence. "So, now what?"

"I'm just waiting for a friend," I said. "I have one who's very good at teaching manners."

Now would be a good time to make an appearance, Pauline, I thought. I glanced over to the top of the hill. No Pauline. Only a slightly flattened Felix, angling at a snail's pace toward the trees. Keep going, kid, I said to myself. Get yourself up a tree before I have to let go.

Mangy's eyes followed mine. "Ha. That pipsqueak? Little Mr. Fluff-N-Stuff? There's not much that midget can teach me."

I shook my head. "Nope. I don't mean Felix. He seems a bit preoccupied at the moment."

The coyote growled but still didn't move. "You're feeding me a line. There's no one out here but the three of us."

I kept my voice confident and cheerful, hoping that Pauline would top the hill any moment. "Oh, I have a *special* friend named Pauline. She's in charge of keeping the residents of this pasture orderly and under control." I looked back at Mangy and forced a grin. "Hey, maybe you've already met her."

Old Mangy stared at me. "I haven't met anyone today."

I flicked an ear and shrugged. "According to Pauline, she had a discussion with someone who looked very much like you—a conversation concerning a lost lamb."

"Ah." Old Mangy took a step backwards, but I was still fastened to his face, so he didn't get very far. "This friend of yours wouldn't happen to be … tall?"

I nodded. "Oh, very. And she has this beautifully long neck that's great for scoping out intruders and a set of marvelously powerful legs that can crush predators with a single blow."

"Uh-huh." Old Mangy couldn't turn his head, but his eyes were busy flicking from side to side. "Well, you're right," he said. "I did have a nice conversation with her, but there's nothing else I need to say. She seems like a very busy lady, so we don't have to bother

her. Now if you'd let me go, I really need to get home before dark."

"Why so soon?" I asked. "Pauline will be disappointed if she doesn't get to talk with you."

"Yeah, I'm sure," the coyote muttered.

"In fact," I said, tilting my head. "I think I hear her coming now."

In fact, I heard nothing of the sort. The only sounds my ears were detecting were the breeze riffling the grass and an overly brave gopher tunneling nearby. But my legs were getting tired. Subterfuge seemed my best bet.

"What?" Old Mangy's tail went rigid. His ears began swiveling round and round.

I pricked my ears. "Yep. I can definitely hear her coming." I glanced at the coyote. "What's wrong? You're looking a little pale underneath that gray coat."

"Nothing. Nothing's wrong," he snapped. "Look, let's just make a deal: You let go. I leave."

"Hmm," I said, tilting my head as if deep in thought. "Here's my offer: I let go. You leave and never come back."

Old Mangy's eyes flashed. "This is a free world. I can come and go as I please."

"Suit yourself," I said, yawning. "I'll just hold on

until Pauline arrives, and she can help us sort this out. She's extremely good at settling disputes."

I could see the whites around Old Mangy's eyes. "You're faking it. She's not really coming."

I shrugged and dug my claws a little deeper into his jowls. "You won't know for sure until she gets here."

Old Mangy froze. From the wild-eyed stare he was giving me, I figured I was in trouble. I sunk my back claws into the ground, steadying myself for his attack.

"OK," he said so suddenly that it almost knocked me backwards.

"What?" I said, trying to keep my fur from poofing.

"OK. I agree. You let go, and I leave and never come back. It's a deal."

I frowned. "Promise?"

"I promise." By now Old Mangy was dancing around as if he'd accidentally jumped into a cactus patch. "On my poor granny's bleached bones, I promise. Now *please* let me go."

His granny's bleached bones hardly seemed convincing enough to me, but I knew I wasn't going to be able to hold on much longer. "At least the lesson in manners worked," I said, slowly relaxing my hold and letting my poor, tired paws drop to the ground.

Old Mangy sat on the grass and swiped at his muzzle. But when he looked over at me again, his eyes had a gleam that made me take a step backwards.

"You promised," I said.

"I promised," he said, jumping to his feet. He snapped at the air just short of my ears, laughed when I shot straight into the air, then turned tail and streaked through the nearby wire fence.

He'd promised.

He'd gone.

I collapsed into an orange puddle, hardly daring to believe it. I'd just fought a coyote—and won!

Chapter Twenty-Two
Here Comes the Cavalry

I'd relaxed for only a few short breaths before a terrible yowl brought me to my feet. My first thought was that Old Mangy had reneged on his promise, bypassed me, and snuck around to attack Felix. I swung my head in the little cat's direction—and saw Pauline. She was walking toward Felix, who was lying poofed and motionless there in the grass.

And then I remembered that Felix had never met Pauline. From Felix's point of view, Pauline was probably just a bigger coyote.

The little cat yowled again.

I bounded forward. "It's okay, Felix. She's a friend." I called.

Pauline stopped and lifted her head.

"George!" she cried, and pulled her lips into as close

a smile as I'd ever seen from her. "Thank goodness you're okay."

I slid to a stop beside her, resisting the urge to rub against her leg and purr. After all, rubbing and purring would be a little unprofessional. "I agree wholeheartedly," I said. Then I turned to Felix, who was doing his best to blend into the stubby grass. "Felix, this is Pauline. She's a friend. A really, really, really good friend."

Felix gazed wide-eyed at the llama.

"Nice to meet you," said Pauline.

Felix continued to stare at her in silence.

She turned back to me. "You must not have run into Old Mangy, then."

"Oh, yeah. We saw him alright." I nodded toward Felix. "And Felix has a set of sore legs to show for it."

Pauline raised her hairy eyebrows. "Then where'd he go?"

I shrugged. "Who knows? Far, far away, I hope. And he promised to never come back, although I wouldn't count on that."

"He just up and *left*?"

"Yep."

"Hmm." She tilted her head. "I have a feeling

there's more to this story, but maybe it should wait until we get home."

"I agree." I glanced at Felix, who'd relaxed enough to start crawling in the direction of the trees again. "But Felix here is going to need some help."

"No, I won't!" Felix hissed. He strained even harder with his front legs, moving from snail's pace to at least turtle's trot. At the speed he was going, it would take him the rest of the day and all night to get home—if he could last that long.

I narrowed my eyes and turned back to Pauline. "Can you carry him?"

She looked down her nose. "Well, I've carried worse. If he can hold on without clawing me."

"Quit talking about me like I'm some bag of kibbles that doesn't care anyway!" Felix spat at us then struggled a little further up the hill.

The kid had gumption, I would give him that. And he was as stubborn as a deaf, blind mule.

"Felix," I said, putting as much authority in my voice as a straggly, bleeding cat can muster. "You'll never make it before you collapse. Take the free ride while you can."

"I can do it myself," Felix snarled at me.

"Yeah, right. Like you handled the coyote yourself?"

"I could've gotten away if you'd left me alone! Now quit giving me orders and go away!"

My fur began to poof. "Listen here—"

"George," Pauline interrupted. "He's exhausted and so are you. Let me handle this." She put her nose next to the floundering cat. "Felix, there are certainly many situations you can handle on your own, but it doesn't make you look bad to accept help from a friend."

Felix went limp and there was silence. Finally he muttered from his heap, "That bossy hairball is certainly not *my* friend." He pulled himself up and began struggling forward again.

Pauline looked at me.

I sighed.

"Felix," I said, but the smaller cat ignored me.

I plopped down in the grass in front of him, blocking his slow escape. "Felix, this situation is mostly my fault."

Felix attempted to change direction, avoiding my eyes. I put out a paw to stop him.

"Hey, I'm attempting to apologize here, and it doesn't happen very often, so listen up!"

The little cat curled into a ball and peered at me

through slitted eyes. "Is that another order?"

"Yes! No." I glared at him, then shut my eyes. "Fine," I said, opening them again. "Please listen."

Felix didn't answer, but at least he stayed put.

I gave my shoulder a few licks to calm myself. "Listen, you tried to sabotage me; I tried to sabotage you. In the end, we both were almost killed. It was only because of my aunt's advice and Pauline's reputation that I was able to save us."

Pauline nodded. "It takes teamwork to make things run smoothly. George and I, we help each other all the time."

I leaned closer. "This is how I see it, kid. This fighting business isn't fun and it isn't working. Maybe we should try getting along instead. You and I could be—you know—friends."

Felix didn't say anything, but his ball seemed to loosen a little.

I pulled the corners of my mouth upward, attempting to smile. "Come on. I've gotta be a better buddy than someone who smells like dog drool."

Felix's whiskers twitched. He turned his head and looked at me for several long breaths. Finally he sighed, "Okay, okay, I'll take the ride."

Pauline knelt beside him, and I helped push him onto her back. Then she carefully climbed to her feet with Felix holding tightly to her neck.

I creaked and groaned, stepping beside them. As we topped the hill, the farmyard seemed to be only a speck in the distance. "Leave it to Old Mangy to pick a spot so far from the barn," I said.

"You're not kidding," answered Pauline. "I'd about given up on finding you until I heard that unearthly howling and yowling. I figured it was your death song."

"It almost was," I said.

Step by careful step, we started down the hill.

I was concentrating on putting one paw in front of the other when Pauline jerked her head upright. "Look at that!"

I looked. A trail of dust was heading toward us. Was it— Could it be—a small vehicle, perhaps?

Within a few seconds, the cloud of dust was close enough that I could see Emma's four-wheeled Mule bouncing along in front of it. Yes, that's right. I said a four-wheeled Mule. I have no idea why humans would use a perfectly good animal name for such a small, jouncy vehicle, but that's just another piece of evidence that humans are a little lacking in the thinking department.

I wasn't going to quibble about name choices, though, when I saw Emma at the wheel with Lil beside her. Twila was holding tightly to Alice in the back seat, and Festus was hanging his head out of the box in the very back. Brutus, almost lost in the cloud of dust, was running beside them.

Pauline and I waited where we were until they lurched to a stop beside us.

Alice immediately squirmed out of Twila's arms and jumped to the ground. "George, are you okay?" Her own hair was standing on end, but she started to lick mine instead.

"Yeah, I'm fine," I said, giving her fur a few swipes of my tongue in return.

She paused and looked at me. "It took me a long time to convince the dogs that something was wrong," she said. "Then it took them awhile to get Lil to realize that Felix was missing." Her whiskers wobbled, and she reapplied her tongue so forcefully to my coat that I could feel patches of hair separating from my neck.

I backed away. "It's okay, Alice. You did great. Thanks for bringing help."

"But you're hurt!"

"I'm fine. Really. This is just a scratch." I nodded toward Pauline. "But Felix is a little beat up."

Alice swung around and gathered her legs under her as if she might spring onto Pauline's back to personally investigate, but Lil had gotten there first.

"Felix!" Lil wailed. "My poor baby. What did that orange cat do to you?"

Felix growled slightly as she reached for him.

"Careful," said Emma, putting up a hand. "I think he's been hurt." She examined the small gray cat. "Hm, I thought so." She pointed to the gashes by Felix's tail. "George didn't do that, Lil. It had to be a critter with bigger teeth." She glanced quickly around the area. "If I'm not mistaken, your cat had a tangle with a coyote. No wonder Pauline brought the sheep to the barn so early."

Emma gave Pauline a pat and gently, gently lifted Felix from his perch. "Come sit in the Mule, Lil, and I'll put him in your lap. We'll get him to the vet."

After Felix had been carefully placed, Emma turned to me. "Let's have a look at you, George." She stroked my head, which I suppose was to distract me while she probed the slash in my side. "This isn't so bad," she said. "As long as you can reach around to lick it clean,

George, I think it'll heal fine."

I gave the wound a swipe with my tongue. Alice gave it another.

Twila laughed. "I'd swear they understand you, Emma."

I narrowed my eyes and muttered to Alice. "And humans think they're so smart."

Emma climbed in the Mule, and Alice and I hopped onto the back seat with Twila.

"I can't stay here anymore," Lil announced suddenly, before Emma could start the engine.

"Of course not," said Emma. "We'll get you back home before you know it. Felix needs a vet."

"No, that's not what I meant," said Lil. When she turned to look at Emma, I could see she was starting to cry again.

What a blubbery human. Even Felix, lying in her lap, looked a little embarrassed.

Lil continued. "I can't live in a place where my animals are continually harassed and attacked. That orange cat is going to be the death of Felix."

Emma took a deep breath.

I cringed. Visions of being shipped off to town floated through my head.

Finally Emma spoke. "Lil, if my eyes aren't deceiving me, this 'orange cat' just saved Felix's life."

What? I thought.

"What?" Lil said.

"Well, look around. If George didn't save Felix from becoming a coyote's supper, who did?"

Lil humphed. "I'd say it was your llama. Isn't that her job?"

"It is," Emma agreed. "But I saw her back at the barn with the sheep just a few minutes before we climbed into the Mule to find Felix. She couldn't have been out here very long before we arrived."

"Then Felix saved himself." Lil crossed her arms. She quickly uncrossed them when Felix growled again.

"It seems your cat might be telling you otherwise." Emma reached down and turned the key. The small vehicle roared to life, and the jiggles and bumps from driving over the rough ground stopped all further conversation.

I laid on the plastic seat and let Twila hold me steady all the way home.

Chapter Twenty-Three
Home Again

I stretched and yawned, opening my eyes and blinking through the sunlight that warmed my napping spot on the porch. The heat sure felt good on stiff muscles. Most of my cuts and bruises had disappeared over the past week, but I was still moving slowly enough that the rodents kept outrunning me. It was downright humiliating.

On the other hand, it was definitely worth the humiliation and pain to have my spot back.

That first day after the coyote attack I'd wandered over to the old porch—just to check on things, of course. Lil had frowned at me, but she hadn't said anything. And when I started coming back each day, she just looked the other way. The really amazing thing was that she kept Felix's food bowl filled, even though she knew perfectly well I was the one eating out of it.

Brutus and Festus weren't giving me any trouble either. When I climbed over the fence, they'd wag their tails politely and move out of the way. The last couple of days they'd even taken to napping on their dog beds in the garage instead of sprawled out on the lawn. Maybe they thought they didn't need to keep an eye on me anymore.

And Felix hadn't been a problem, of course, because he'd spent the entire week at the vet. Lil had gone into town every day to check on him and had come back every day without him. I knew I couldn't do anything to help him heal faster, so I did the only thing I *could* do: I enjoyed the sunny spot for him.

As I flopped over to continue my nap, Lil's car pulled into the yard. I turned my head and watched her remove a cat carrier from the back seat, and for the first time this week, it wasn't empty. A gray shape crouched inside.

I pulled myself to a seated position and watched as Lil brought the carrier up the porch steps. She set it down carefully but didn't open the door. I stiffened as she looked at me. She wasn't smiling, but she wasn't frowning, either. Her eyebrows were pulled together as though she was wondering what to do.

Well, there was no time like the present to be friendly. I put my tail in the air and rubbed against her leg, adjusting the volume of my purr so that she would be sure to feel it vibrate. I wished that Alice were here to evaluate my technique. She'd been giving me lessons in how to persuade humans, but this was my first real opportunity to give it a try.

Lil studied me for a few seconds then shook her head. I turned up the volume until my purr was almost a roar. Lil shook her head again, and I thought I was done for. But then she bent and opened the carrier door.

I dipped my head to peer through the opening. Felix was hunkered down way in the back, staring at me.

"Come on out, Felix," Lil coaxed. But Felix stayed put.

Lil glanced at me. She knew as well as I did why Felix wouldn't come out. I tensed, ready for her to toss me into the bushes.

Instead she shrugged. "Felix, you're just going to have to learn how to get along with George. He was here first after all, and Emma says he's a very smart cat. It'd be good to have him looking out for you." With that, she took a deep breath and stood. Then she pulled open the screen door and went into the house, leaving Felix and me alone together.

I stared at the door, half expecting to see Lil lurking there, ready to pound me if I made any sudden moves. But I couldn't see her through the screen's mesh. She was really and truly gone.

I turned back to Felix. He was still staring at me. Briefly, I wondered if he could see my swelled head. It sure felt nice to know I was appreciated. I opened my mouth, ready to order him out of that box so we could talk. Then I shut it again and took a breath. I twitched my tail and concentrated on the words I'd been rehearsing with Alice.

"Hey, kid. Welcome home. I saved you a spot!" I scooted over and nodded to the patch of sun.

He looked at me, his ears pricking forward as if he weren't sure he'd heard quite right.

I tucked my tail around my feet and gave another friendly nod toward the spot beside me. "Why don't you come on over here, youngster?" I said. "I'd sure like to give this another try. My name's George, by the way, and I'm the farm cat hired on for rodent patrol around here. What do they call you?"

Felix slowly rose from his crouch but kept his eyes fixed on me as he eased himself out of the crate.

I grinned at him, and he gave me a hesitant whisker twitch in return. Then I nodded my head toward the puddle of sun once more. "There's plenty of room here, if you'd like."

Ever so carefully, the little gray cat lowered himself into the warmth beside me. "My name's Felix," he said.

"Glad to meet you, Felix," I said. "I'm hoping that we can be friends."

Little by little, Felix's face relaxed. He curled his tail around himself in a pose similar to mine. "Me, too," he said.

A warm feeling spread through me, and it wasn't from the sun, if you know what I mean.

Just then, Brutus stuck his nose out of the garage. "Hey, Festus. The boss is back!" And he rushed for the porch.

I heard a couple of happy yips and yaps from the garage, and then Festus burst out of the door, ears trailing behind him.

Felix rubbed a paw over his own ear and glanced sideways at me before turning to watch the dogs bound up the steps. "Hi, guys," he said.

The bruisers slid to a stop and began licking their small friend's fur and tattooing him with their tails.

"Hey, stop it," the kid laughed. "Stop it, okay? I can't breathe."

The dogs instantly sat.

"Right, Boss," said Festus.

"Um." Felix glanced at me again. "The 'boss' stuff isn't necessary anymore, guys. I think we're getting this worked out."

"What a relief," said Brutus, flopping down. "It's been a little hard keeping up the act with that Eloise gal prattling on and on about being neighborly."

I could feel my fur getting a little ruffled. "Act? What act?"

"We-e-e-ll." Felix hesitated.

Festus nudged the small cat with his nose, and Felix sighed.

"It's like this," he said. "The very first day we moved here, Jason built the cat door so that I could go in and out of the house as I pleased, but Lil had a fit. She wanted to keep me locked in the house like she had back in our old apartment." He looked down at the ground.

"And?" I prompted.

Felix rubbed a paw over his face. "And she kept telling Jason that it wasn't safe for me outside with that huge terror of a cat, George, wandering around. She rattled on and on about how big you were and how mean you were and … well … the thought of meeting you scared me so much that I asked the boys …" He nodded to the dogs. "I asked them to pretend that I was the boss. I figured if it looked like I was giving them orders, you'd think I was too tough to handle."

The little cat shook his head and looked up at me. "It was all an act—a stupid, stupid act."

I opened my mouth to agree wholeheartedly with how stupid he'd been but was momentarily interrupted by Ted's truck rumbling out of the yard with a full load of hay. My mouth snapped shut and I took a deep breath. "Listen, kid, don't come down on yourself too hard. I pulled some stunts, too. Like the business about me walking into town."

Felix tilted his head. "What about it?"

"I didn't really walk. I accidentally rode along in a load of hay and got stranded there."

"Oh."

"Yeah." My whiskers twitched. "*I* was trying to look

tough to discourage *you*. It didn't work so hot for me, either."

Felix widened his eyes. "I guess not."

"I'm hoping it will work better this way."

"Me, too." Felix looked away, toward the barn. "George?"

"Yeah?"

"Alice said you were really good at teaching her how to hunt mice."

"Well, uh …" I drew myself up a little taller.

"Would you teach me, too?"

I curved my whiskers upward. "You really want to learn?"

"I really want to learn."

"Sure," I said. "I'd be happy to."

"Good. Thank you."

The little cat curled up next to me and closed his eyes.

I closed my eyes, too, basking in the sun's warmth on my back. Where should I take the kid first? The grain bins? The garden? The barn?

I cracked my eyes open just enough to study the sleeping cat beside me. It didn't matter where we went first. I'd let the little guy choose. We'd work together.

We'd be a great team.

Watch out mice, I thought, stretching out on the porch beside the other sleeping animals. You won't be outrunning me much longer. And next time you see me, I'll be bringing along a friend.

Another farm cat has arrived.

Acknowledgements

This book would certainly not have come to you in readable form if not for the help of some very strong-willed people.

Many thanks goes to my family—my parents for encouraging me, my husband, Kris, for taking care of chores and kids and even allowing me to quit my "real" job so that I would have time to write, and my kids, Isaac and Miriam, for being excited to hear George's story again and again even though they probably wondered if I would ever get done with it.

Thanks to my writing sisters, Rebecca Johnson, Val Padmore, and Beth Summers for reading and rereading, commenting, haranguing, and making me toe the line. (You're the best writing group a person could have!) Also thanks to my original bunch of readers, Nancy Wagner, Jean Patrick, and Carolyn Zeisset for encouraging me through the first rough draft.

Much appreciation goes to Cindy Johnson and Patty Johnston for reading the book in manuscript form to their students at school and collecting comments for me. I'm also grateful to Leslie Dickman for allowing me to visit her llamas and patiently explaining llama behavior to me. Thanks to first grader (and cat lover), Lena Spencer, for keeping me on track by frequently asking (at least once a week) if my cat book was done yet. And I'm very appreciative of Beth Summers and Jean Cox for being willing to read the manuscript closely for editing purposes.

Last, but certainly not least, a big thank you to Nancy Wagner, my publisher, who has been my companion through the novel writing process from beginning to end. I'm so glad that you were willing to share the journey!

Made in the USA
Columbia, SC
23 February 2020